W9-BEW-053

DEVILISH

Devilish

MAUREEN JOHNSON

HarperCollins*Publishers*

First published in hardback in the USA by G. P. Putnam's Sons,
a division of Penguin Young Readers Group in 2006
First published in paperback in Great Britain by HarperCollins *Children's Books* in 2012
HarperCollins *Children's Books* is a division of HarperCollins*Publishers* Ltd,
77–85 Fulham Palace Road, Hammersmith, London, W6 8JB.

The HarperCollins website address is: www.harpercollins.co.uk

1

Copyright © 2006 by Maureen Johnson

Published by arrangement with Razorbill, a division of Penguin Young Reader's Group,
a member of Penguin Group (USA) Inc.

ISBN 978-0-00-748451-5

Maureen Johnson asserts the moral right to be identified as the author of the work.

Set in Sabon Ltd Std by Palimpsest Book Production Limited,
Falkirk, Stirlingshire

Printed and bound in England by Clays Ltd, St Ives plc

Conditions of Sale
This book is sold subject to the condition that it shall not,
by way of trade or otherwise, be lent, re-sold, hired out or otherwise circulated
without the publisher's prior consent in any form, binding or cover other than
that in which it is published and without a similar condition including this condition
being imposed on the subsequent purchaser. All rights reserved.

MIX
Paper from
responsible sources
FSC
www.fsc.org FSC® C007454

FSC™ is a non-profit international organisation established to promote
the responsible management of the world's forests. Products carrying the
FSC label are independently certified to assure consumers that they come
from forests that are managed to meet the social, economic and
ecological needs of present and future generations,
and other controlled sources.

Find out more about HarperCollins and the environment at
www.harpercollins.co.uk/green

For J.W. Keeley, my little piece of hell on earth, and my friend for all eternity. And Mr. Jones, wherever he may be.

Prologue

So this was how it ended. The revelers had deserted, leaving plates of Spanish almonds and sushi and cupcake wrappers. Now there would be no more grand ballrooms with Assyrian kings and pampered dogs and English pop stars and the A3. No more midnight rides through the skies of Providence. No more Calculus II with Brother Frank. No more stolen moments with 116-year-old boys or staring at the golden brick mansion across the fields. It had come back to this mad room of antique perfume bottles and disagreements.

Only a handful of people would understand the real meaning of this event. The general public would be horror-struck. They would wonder how two best friends, two otherwise unassuming girls on the verge of adulthood, could have ended up like this. There would be new specials and magazine articles: 'Teen Tragedy Stuns Providence,' 'Rhode Island Rampage.' I would be cast as the brainy troublemaker — the angry little blond punk. Allison would be portrayed as my sweet, devoted friend — the one I had tricked and mislead and taken down this tragic path. The real villain would not appear in the stories at all.

Oh, I had no doubt that they'd blame the whole mess on me, probably just because I had spiky hair and a tendency to talk too much. That was the story of my life. And that life was over.

It doesn't matter how old you are when you die, I'd been told. When you die, that's the right time for you. I'd also been told my life was a small price to pay.

I was glad to pay it for Allison.

My hand fell away from the phone. The room grew dark and I felt myself slipping down the side of the sofa, down to the prized Oriental rug. This was my final move in the game, this graceless thud to the floor. There was only one question left in my mind...

Had I played it right?

two weeks earlier...

Chapter 1

The reviews from the Junior Judges had gone up on the website in the middle of the night. This was how they described me:

> JARVIS, JANE; CLASSROOM 2A: If you are trying to find Jane Jarvis, look down. Jane is the shortest person at St. Teresa's, the littlest big. But that tiny body contains a huge brain. We must give this to her. Famously argumentative — we all remember fondly Jane's impromptu speech during last year's 'Celebration of the Spirit of Womanhood' assembly, when she openly debated with the visiting bishop about the rights of women in the church. We like a little less her brittle, bleach blond spikes. A retro no-no in our book. If you are the angry, brainy type, consider Jane. She can be your personal Yoda.

Nothing new there. I went right on to Allison's. The first word struck me, and it was all downhill from there:

CONCORD, ALLISON; CLASSROOM 1A: Forehead first...
Allison Concord has a showstopper. We have never
seen anything quite like it. It's kind of like an unused
billboard or a makeshift landing strip at a small
midwestern airport. Sexy. Comparable only to her
gums, which are truly a sight to behold. The pinkest
smile we've ever seen. She is best known for counting
down every second to the junior prom — and then
showing up without a date and looking very boo-hoo.
Tragic. If you haven't got anyone else for your big
and no one else will take on a second...Well, we do
what we must.

When there is blood on the water, the sharks will rise to
the surface. And Big-Little Day, our yearly celebration of
sisterhood, was one of the bloodiest days of the year.

Big-Little Day was a major school benchmark when
seniors would officially ask a freshman or a new
underclassman to be their 'little.' Enterprising freshmen
would actively campaign the most popular seniors, leaving
notes and tokens and generally sucking up in a really gross
manner. It was a massively big deal to have a good little.
Any self-respecting senior, it was understood, had to have
at least three freshmen courting them. A few luminaries
might have eight or ten offers. And selection was rapid.
There was only one forty-five minute period at the start
of the day to get it all done. By the end, we were expected
to pull off our class rings and pass them to our chosen
freshmen, who got to wear them for a day — making the
whole thing a little creepily marriage-like as well.

The buildup to this event had been going on since school had started... clandestine meetings in the bathroom between classes, lunchtime congresses, a fury of note taking and illegal texting. But the really serious part was the evaluation by the Junior Judges, a group of self-nominated juniors who offered commentary on all the seniors on the day itself.

No one knew who the first Junior Judges were. The tradition was known to go back as far as the eighties. Back then, they got their message out using photocopied sheets that they stuck in all the freshman lockers. And every year since then, a group of juniors rose up and took on the task.

Even though they were self-chosen, the Junior Judges were hardly anonymous. This year's group was a trio who called themselves the A3. The reason for this is so painfully pretentious that I can barely write it down, and if I really sit down and figure out how it is I even know this, something bad will happen to my head. So I won't do that. I will simply explain that it comes from a size of paper in England called A3, which is really long paper. One of them went to England and discovered this, and they all started joking about how they liked 'really long paper,' as if that actually means something. Combine that with the fact that *A* generally means the best and the fact that there are three of them: Elsie Fast, Tracey Pils, and Lai Barden. It all comes together into one ready-made nickname. (Awful things like that tend to converge. Know that and you'll be ahead of the game.)

These were the people digging up the past that I had

worked all summer long to bury and cover in concrete. I had gone so far as to turn down a summer job helping to compile research data for my dad at his office at Brown, where he's a professor. It had taken a lot for me to get that job in the first place — including a two-hour interview in which I had to prove that I knew enough math to handle it. And I gave it up. Instead, I made my money at the same summer job that Ally and I had always worked, scooping ice cream in a four-by-five foot fluorescent cell at Dibney's. But this is what you do when your best friend needs you, even if it means chucking away an opportunity that could help you score a scholarship to college.

And the A3 may have just undone it all, simply by being their snarky, haggish selves.

My sister, Joan, was picking all of the green and orange pieces out of her bowl of Froot Loops when I came downstairs. Spread out in front of her were some books and papers. Joan never actually did her homework. I'm not sure Joan actually *knew* that she was supposed to do it — I think she may have been under the impression that she was just supposed to watch over it for the night and make sure nothing happened to it. Every morning, she took it out and checked to make sure that every page was as blank, every problem was as undone, and every answer was just as unwritten as when she'd first taken it under her wing.

'What's a parallelogram?' she asked, peering at her textbook through two Loops she held up to her eyes.

My father was too busy poking at a Sudoku puzzle

to answer. He couldn't leave the house until he did one of the hard ones in under two minutes. My mother never joined our breakfast group because she was always asleep. She worked late managing a very fancy and very good restaurant in town called The Pink Peppercorn, providing us with the world's best leftovers. Which is why I was having a bowl of cold sirloin tips for breakfast.

'It's a four-sided plane,' I said. 'The opposite sides are parallel.'

'A four-sided *plane*?' she repeated. 'Okay, I am *not* falling for that one.'

Joan is two years younger than me. She didn't get into St. Teresa's Preparatory School for Girls. I'm completely used to her looking up at me with that lip-glossy stare of hers and asking questions like, 'Is the Tour de France in Spain?' or, 'Do they make cotton out of plastic?' This is a girl who I had convinced that Alaska used to be called Frigidaire. So sometimes she thought I lied to her.

My father smiled and shook his head. It never bothered him that Joan was like that. While she didn't get my father's savage intelligence or my mother's dexterous common sense, she did get all the height, the muscle tone, and the strong and shiny brown hair. She was lovely and happy, even if she was as intelligent as a rubber band.

Whereas I, as the Junior Judges had so rightly pointed out, was four-foot ten and five-sixths inches (in school shoes) with blond hair, and I looked like an escaped street urchin from *Oliver Twist*. (The hair was dry and brittle because I dyed it with a home-brewed peroxide solution, which worked really well when I first started doing it as a freshman and couldn't stop because if I used anything else on my hair, it turned a kind of moss-green color.)

Joan set her Froot Loops down and gazed at me evenly.

'You have that look on your face,' she said. 'Are you thinking about Elton?'

My dad glanced up from his puzzle.

'No.' I gave her a silencing look, stiffening my jaw. She knew she wasn't supposed to mention my ex in front of my dad because he would think I was still upset. It had been six months, three weeks, and two days since our breakup. I was over it.

'It's Allison, I said. 'Today is Big-Little Day. I need to make sure she gets a little. This is the first big event since the prom. It means a lot to her. I can't let anything bad happen.'

'Allison will be fine,' my dad chimed in. 'Why would you need to worry about her?'

This was one thing Joan understood completely.

'Ally needs to relax,' Joan said. 'Someone will definitely take her as long as she doesn't get all... you know... spazzy.'

'How do you keep someone from being spazzy?' I asked, pushing aside some mushrooms that had attached themselves to the steaky goodness. 'I know she's great, but she's going to be wound up today. She's going to start breathing fast and get dizzy and scare away the freshmen.'

'You can't worry about something that hasn't happened yet,' my father said, turning back to his Sudoku. 'You have to take life as it comes.'

This irritated me. When I worry about one thing, I

frequently take it out on something or someone else. And the fact that my dad was offering stupid and totally untrue advice set me off.

'Oh no?' I said. 'Isn't worrying about things that haven't happened yet the purpose of several major government agencies, like the army and FEMA? What about yearly checkups? Savings accounts? Tornado shelters? Earthquake-proofing?'

'Moisturizer?' Joan added.

'You're a math professor,' I said. 'What the study of probability? Figuring out what will *probably* happen. And then you dump all of that probability information into huge tables that insurance companies use. So they know who will probably crash their car, which places will probably get flooded, who might trip into the fireplace and set themselves on fire...'

'I don't think there's a category for that, Jane.'

'You see my point,' I said archly. 'Of *course* we know bad things do happen. And I know that Allison is probably going to spaz. She will probably start talking about her collection of Build-A-Bears or quoting entire episodes of *Charmed*, and while I think she's cute, most people will think she's insane and they will run.'

I was getting a little frenzied now. Joan was nodding away, like I was preaching and she had been infected by the spirit — but my dad was still back a few steps.

'But she hasn't done any of that yet,' he said. 'If you go into it with that attitude, there's almost no point. Probability isn't a guarantee. Give her some credit. You have to assume that she'll do just fine.'

'But she *won't*.'

'Well, then,' my dad said, quietly folding his completed puzzle in half, 'sounds like she had no chance in the first place. So I guess…'

He stood and flicked a lost Froot Loop over at Joan.

'…you'll just have to save her from herself.'

Chapter 2

The sky was red that morning, which I think is supposed to be a sailor's warning about something… storms, waves, sea monsters. It was a stupidly hot morning, too. October in Providence, Rhode Island, is not a hot time, normally. It's New England — we like it cold and grim. We cultivate colds like some areas of the world nurture grapes and produce fine wines.

There was no homeroom for us. We were all instructed to go right to the gym, where folding tables had already been set up all along the walls. Where we, the seniors, were supposed to sit. The freshmen and new students would all stream in and approach us.

My fears turned out to be for nothing. Instead of the weepy Ally I was expecting, she walked in proudly examining a red velvet cupcake at arm's length, displaying it to me.

'I found it in my locker,' she said with a grin. 'With this.'

She held up a note that read: WILL YOU BE MY BIG?

'Some freshman must be trying to suck up to you!' I said with enthusiasm. 'Would have helped if she'd left her *name*. But points for busting into your locker to leave you cake.'

She broke it in half and offered a piece to me, then immediately withdrew it and hid it behind her back.

'Sorry,' she said. 'Red chocolate. I wasn't thinking.

I can't eat red foods. They freak me out. No food should be the color of blood.

There was a warning squawk of the microphone, so Allison crammed the rest of the cupcake into her mouth, getting a little frosting on her cheek in the process. I felt bad about doubting her that morning. Allison was a big girl — she could handle herself.

'Today's your day,' I said. 'I can feel it. You're doing a lot better than me. I got squat.'

'Someone will come for you,' she said. 'Everyone *knows* you.'

Our vice principal, Sister Dominic, came up to the microphone to lead us through a Hail Mary; two specially written appeals to St. Teresa, begging her to help us all become better sisters; and one verse of 'Join Us Together with a Rainbow of Love,' a hymn written by a former student of questionable sanity. Then our student counsel president, Donna Skal, went to the microphone in the middle of the room.

'Good morning, St. T.'s!' she said, much, much too loudly. 'A little warm in here today, huh? Must be all of that big-little energy!'

We were roasting in our polyester uniforms, yanking desperately at our collars, and twisting to find more air.

'Sisterhood,' Donna went on. 'What does it mean?'

'It usually means having a sister,' I said to Ally in a low voice.

'Would you shut up?' she whispered. 'They'll kick us out, and then I won't get a little.'

'I can't help it,' I said. 'I'm allergic to people who talk like spokesmodels.'

This wasn't really fair. There was nothing particularly wrong with Donna, except for the fact that she was successful because she had that odd squeaky-cleanness that lots of teen pop stars exude, the kind that seems to have been manufactured in a laboratory. Her hair was genuinely golden, and her eyes were large, like a cartoon deer's. She could sometimes be heard saying things like, 'My sister told me I laugh in my sleep!' (The best I've ever gotten from my sister was, 'I thought there was something wrong with the dog, but it was just you snoring.')

'Sisterhood means loving each other no matter what we look like or how we dress outside of school,' Donna explained. 'Sisterhood means putting each other first. Sisterhood means believing in each other and going the extra mile.'

'Or it means having a sister,' I added quickly.

Ally giggled before she could stop herself and shoved her fist into her mouth, but she was a hair too late. Sister Dominic lifted herself up on her toes and scanned the seniors. She found us quickly. She held two fingers up in the air and then poked a finger first at me, then at Ally. I knew this gesture well. It translated into two demerits, each of you. Ally let out a low groan.

'Sorry,' I whispered.

One of the doors in the back opened. We all heard it, and everyone turned in unison.

'There they are,' Ally said, suddenly awed.

In a minute of shuffling and whispering, the freshmen were lined up like an advancing army, all with bright, crazy looks in their eyes. We quickly assumed our positions in the chairs. A jumpy, almost volatile vibe came into the room, and the temperature shot up about ten degrees.

'And now,' Donna said, 'the big-little ceremony begins!'

The first flank of freshmen broke free and literally ran at us, targeting very specific people. They charged at Donna, who actually opened her arms to welcome them, like some kind of mother goddess.

'I can't watch,' I said. But I did anyway.

A group with the easy stride of athletes made their way to Brooke Makepeace, the understated captain of the basketball team. There was a lot of giggling and near-skipping to Hillary Vorpel, school musical diva and former child star (of local theaters and supposedly 'a very big show in New York' that was never named). Within a minute, she was blinding four freshmen with her laser whites. We were sitting next to Kristin Durkin, who had no real portfolio except for being nice and kind of pretty, a good safety choice. Within a minute, she had two applicants.

'Where is she?' Allison asked, glaring at Kristin's short line. 'Why hasn't she come up to me?'

'Give it a minute,' I said. 'There's still some in the back.'

The next wave was a slower, more considered group. They made their way to the next tier — not the superstars, but the perfectly acceptable people. The everyone elses. This was a slow, trickle-down kind of thing.

'No one's coming over here,' Allison said. Her voice sounded odd. She was suddenly gruff, almost angry-sounding. I turned to find that she had gone a little bit gray. She was sweating, but then everyone else was, too. But she was also gripping the edge of her folding desk with an intensity that couldn't be good.

'Hey, Al,' I said. 'Are you okay?'

'I'm fine,' she said tersely.

The mysterious little didn't come. Ten agonizing minutes went by. Allison watched the room and watched the clock. I watched Allison. She was naturally pretty pale, but now she was turning a color kind of like freezer-burned bread: not quite gray, not quite blue, not quite bread. Not a good shade to be. It started at her chin and zipped right up her head, right to her hairline — and that's kind of a long way. I couldn't take it anymore.

'You're not okay,' I said. 'You need to get some air. Just tell them you don't feel good.'

'I'll be *fine*,' she said, clenching her teeth. 'I'm just hot. I have to get a little.'

I became aware of a buzzing, which I at first thought was the undertow of all the conversations going on. I looked around, but all that was in front of me was a mob of schmooze. I don't know why I looked up. I just did. That's when I saw them... the flies. Hundreds of them were streaming in through the open windows. Most had gone right for the ceiling and were dripping down like icicles. I had never seen so many flies. There were entire constellations of them.

My hand automatically went out to tap Allison and point this out, but then I realized that this might not be good, not the way she was feeling. I looked around to see if anyone else saw this or if the heat had just driven me insane.

There was a loud scraping noise of a chair being pushed back. It echoed through the gym and caused many people to turn, including me. The sound came from directly next to me. It was Allison, leaping up from her seat. She was obviously trying to cut through the room and get to the door, but she ran straight into a freshman who was slowly and deliberately coming in the direction of Ally or me or Kristin.

Then Ally threw up.

Well, it was more than that, unfortunately. It was truly projectile, and it was accompanied by horrible coughing noises that almost sounded like barking. She got the poor freshman completely and totally, mostly in the hair.

For a second, there was no sound. Then there was a loud intake of breath and a sound of awe. A few higher-pitched squeaks. People backed up and moved away. The freshman let out a wail the likes of which I have never heard before. It was a real end-of-the-world scream. This stirred the room and sound increased — cries of sympathetic horror from all corners, as if Allison had just thrown up on everyone in the gym, everyone in the world. A few people rushed toward the freshman to help. No one was quite able to bring themselves to touch her — most pulled out tissues or anything they had on them and passed them to the girl.

No one reached out to help Ally except for me and one of the sisters who was standing nearby. Allison pulled away from us and ran for it. The crowd parted for her, and she was gone.

Chapter 3

'It's not that bad,' I lied.

I could see the soles of Allison's saddle shoes poking out from under the pink stall door, toes to the ground. Classic puking position. But she wasn't sick anymore — she was dead silent. I poked at the sole of one of her shoes with my foot. Nothing.

'People will forget,' I added. 'They're all too busy.'

Nothing.

'And not everyone saw it.' I was talking stupidly now, relentlessly, just to fill the air. Everyone saw it. Everyone would remember it for all time. It would be written into the fossil record.

I heard voices outside as people left the assembly and started to repopulate the halls. I heard cries of excitement. Just outside the bathroom door, freshmen were showing each other rings. Outside, there was joy. It was at that moment I realized I also hadn't gotten a little. The shock and awe of what happened to Ally had stunned me briefly.

But now, now I saw it — and it hit me harder than I imagined it would.

Help Ally, my good inner Jane told me. *You didn't really care that much about getting a little.*

'You want me to run down to the café and get you a ginger ale?' I asked.

Finally, a reply.

'I want you,' she said, 'to kill me.'

The bathroom door opened, and a very tall girl slipped inside. She was long. Easily six feet, one of which was all neck. The blue stripe on her blazer pocket told me she was a sophomore. The blazer looked very squeaky-new, and I'd never seen her before. She was the kind of person you would remember if you saw.

'Hey,' the girl said. She didn't look like she'd come in for any real purpose — just one of those time-killer visits. She stood in front of the mirror and minutely adjusted the bands that held her two rust-red ponytails in place. Then she turned and looked at Ally's shoe bottoms.

'That was an interesting assembly,' she said to the mirror. 'I didn't think anything cool would happen here, but that was pretty good.'

Together we looked down at Allison's shoes. They did not reply, but the left heel did sink towards the ground a bit.

'I'm new,' the girl said. 'That's why I was there. I'm Lanalee. Lanalee Tremone.'

The warning bell rang. The shoes didn't budge. I got down on my knees and peered under the door. Ally was resting with her head on the seat and a blank look on her face.

'Shouldn't she go home?' Lanalee asked.

'They don't really let us go home here,' I said, poking my hand under the door and stroking Ally's ankle in a pathetic attempt to comfort her. 'You pretty much have to be dead. And even then I think they'd just keep your body in the front office until the end of the day.'

The shoes shifted a little and drew themselves out of reach.

'Do you think you can make it to English, Al?' I asked. 'We have to go or we'll be late.'

One hoarse word of reply:

'Go.'

'I don't want to go without you. Sister Charles will freak.'

'Go.'

'Can you come out?'

'Go.'

I got to my feet. The girl leaned down and addressed the opening under the door gently.

'Did you get a little?' she asked.

I heard a slight shifting from inside the stall, but no answer was forthcoming. I shook my head.

'Well, you can have me,' she said brightly. 'I didn't get a big. There!'

This was an amazingly generous offer, considering. I'm not proud to say that it only highlighted the fact that I was still little-less.

'I'll stay with her,' the girl offered. 'I wasn't planning on going to next period anyway.'

I didn't really want to leave, but there wasn't much I could do. Sister Charles had never actually killed anyone, but she did leave you with the feeling that she was capable of some deeply frightening behavior.

'Okay,' I said. 'I'll go and tell her you'll be late. Okay, Al?'

Nothing.

'Go on,' the girl said. 'Really. Let me bond with my big.'

And so I left the bathroom, just as the second bell rang. I got a demerit from Sister Rose Marie for running in the hallway between classes for my trouble.

Chapter 4

Sister Charles was old enough to have figured prominently in some of the later Bible stories. She was constantly angry, and it took her forever to get down the hall. The reason for these last two was that she had no big toes.

How she lost her big toes was kind of a mystery, but when you have no big toes, it ruins your sense of balance and causes you to walk in circles. It doesn't help when you are already old and generally a little nuts and you have to walk with a three-pronged cane. The added insult of walking in circles all the time makes you hate the teenage girls you teach — because you already think they are lazy and dumb and sex-obsessed and illiterate — so you are furious from the moment you wake up in the morning that big toes are wasted on them. I guess, to be fair, I'd be a little edgy too if it took me five hours to cross the soccer field because I just kept looping and looping and looping. But still, I wouldn't take it out on innocent youth.

This is who we spent the first period of every day

with. Her class, English, was also the only class that Ally and I had together this year. I took mostly AP and special classes, but this English class was the only one that fit my schedule.

I opened the door as carefully as I could, but I don't know why I bothered. It wasn't like Sister Charles wasn't going to notice that I was late. She wheeled on me.

'Did you not hear the bell?' she asked. 'At this school, when girls hear the bell, they proceed to class.'

'Yes, Sister,' I said, heading right for my desk. 'I was with Allison. She's sick.'

'You are a doctor?' she asked curiously.

A ripple of movement, submerged laughter, went around the room. It made my skin go cold, even in the painful heat. Sister noticed this and looked around.

'She's very sick,' I said, keeping my eyes only on Sister.

'She is. We all saw her. She was throwing up in the assembly.' This was from Donna, who was also in the class. Somehow, being student counsel president gave her the ability to verify things. She did it all the time. Homework assignments, weather conditions, days of the week, pages we left off on. Donna was happy to tell us all.

Sister was about to reply when the door creaked open once more and Allison pressed her way through about six inches of opening. She was totally and truly white — almost blue.

'I understand you have been ill,' Sister said. 'Is that so?'

Allison froze, still in the crack of the doorway. All

31

eyes turned to her. She put her hand on the door, high enough that it was clear to see that she was not wearing her ring. At the very least, she was going to show the room that she had managed to get herself a little.

Nothing *actually* happened. No one *actually* said anything. The earth does not have to split open and a thousand-foot gulch does not have to appear for you to know that someone has been cast out. Especially if that someone has never really been in. I'm sure if some behavioral scientists filmed the room and watched the footage they'd be able to point out some things. The way some people looked mildly repulsed, as if they could still smell vomit. The way Donna had a completely inappropriate smile. The way some people didn't even bother to turn at all, and just looked at the diagram of an introductory paragraph on the board and pressed their lips together, trying not to laugh. The way Allison walked to her desk as if she didn't belong on the planet, as if she wanted to apologize for her existence. The spell on the room was total. Even Sister Charles seemed fascinated by it. She went right back to the lesson with no further comment, which was very telling. The pressure in the room actually *hurt*.

Which is why I did what I did next.

We had many stupid rules at St. Teresa's, but one that I really couldn't stand was that — no matter how hot it was — the most we could ever do to cool ourselves was take off our blazers. We couldn't roll up our long sleeves, push down our woolen kneesocks, open our shirts another button or untuck them. So I did *all* of these things, slowly, deliberately, and as broadly as I could get away with. I unbuttoned my cuffs, rolled the sleeves to the elbow, reached down and pushed down the socks, loosened my collar.

And it worked. Slowly, attention went away from Ally and over to me. Even as I was doing it, I was dreading Sister Charles's long, loaded silence. A stifled giggle came from behind me. But I kept on doing it, drawing out each gesture as long as I could.

Finally, when I had reached the point where I'd actually have to strip if I wanted to go any further, Sister Charles decided to speak.

'Are you warm, Miss Jarvis?' she said politely.

'Kind of, Sister,' I said loudly.

A laugh now from the front.

'I think we are all warm. Yet we remain clothed. But perhaps an exception should be made for you?'

'I was just doing what seemed sensible, Sister.'

I had engaged her now. Sister smiled slightly. It looked unnatural on her, like mascara on a baby.

'Well, Miss Jarvis, you may have a point.' She crossed around the desk in a loopy path. 'Do you have your PE outfit in your bag?'

I stiffened. Our PE kit consisted of a very tight and unflattering T-shirt, with the world's shortest, most terrifying shorts. Lap dancers wouldn't wear our shorts. Our school made us dress extremely conservatively, but for gym, tiny tees and butt-kerchiefs were considered healthy. It was a trauma, but it was a trauma we went through together, and it never left the gym.

'I would like you to go to the ladies' room and put

it on,' she said. 'You will wear it for the rest of the day. I will call the office and let them know this is acceptable. Please do keep your school shoes on, though.'

I rose with all the dignity I could muster, smiled at the people who snickered, and made my way to the bathroom.

Chapter 5

I spent the rest of the day walking around school in tiny shorts, kneesocks, and saddle shoes. Ally was nowhere to be found. It would have been completely understandable if she was avoiding me. It was hard to believe that I could have compounded the problem — but no one will ever say that Jane Jarvis isn't an innovator.

Calculus II was my last class of the day. I had it with only one other person, Cassie Malloy. It was kind of a special thing; they offered it just to us. We didn't even use a classroom. We sat in Brother Frank's office, which was no more than an elaborate broom closet on the third floor, just big enough for a desk and two chairs. Still, the intimacy gave it a real scholastic feel.

Cassie took in my outfit in a brief glance and decided not to comment.

'Oh my God,' she said. 'Who did you get? Oh my God. You probably got, like, five offers. I only got one, and I don't even think she knew who I was. Are you going to spend a lot of time with yours? Because I have, like, *no time* right now.'

She reached into her bag, pulled out a slim thermos, and took a long gulp of coffee. The caffeine was no good for her — it made her hands shake mildly. But she needed it. Cassie didn't sleep. She was a hard worker. I had long speculated that she would be dead by thirty in an attempt to do medical and law school at the same time.

'How late were you up doing this?' she asked, flipping through her notebook, through page after page of neatly written equations. Cassie did them in order, step by step, six to a page. I pulled out my own work — a collection of scribblings written on some paper from our printer's recycling box.

'Oh… a while,' I lied, looking at the work I had done while watching TV.

At least Cassie wasn't asking me about Allison. I wasn't sure she was asking me anything. She produced a pen from her wildly sproingy hair and hurriedly scribbled something in her Filofax while she was talking. Whether I was there or not was probably irrelevant.

'They do this at the *worst* time. I mean, I'm doing SATs again on Saturday. Fourth time. God! Are you doing them again? I seriously have no time to spend with this girl. I'm just going to get her a teddy bear or something and that's it. Do you like yours?'

And then, Cassie screamed, a particularly high-pitched, nerve-jangling scream. Which made me scream. Screams are catchy. I followed Cassie's gaze to a tiny black-veiled head in the doorway.

'I see PANTIES!' it shrieked. 'I see blue panties!'

Cassie clapped her legs tightly together. The head snapped out of sight.

'God,' she wheezed. 'Why does she do that?'

Sister Rose Marie would pop her head into classrooms at random, examine the horizon, and look for people sitting in a manner that exposed underwear. This shock attack was supposed to make us more ladylike. It just made us paranoid. For one moment that day, I was glad to be wearing my shorts.

Brother Frank, our teacher, came in. I liked Brother Frank the most out of all my teachers. He was brilliant, for a start, and Irish (though his accent flitted in and out like bad radio reception), and he had a shock of gray hair that stuck up straight from his head, the way really good mathematicians should.

Something was wrong today, though — his huge salt-and-pepper eyebrows were knitting themselves together and unwinding again. He dropped himself down in his chair heavily.

'Cassie,' he said. 'Sister Charles needs some help this period. She isn't feeling well because of all the heat. She need someone to watch over her freshman English class for a period while they workshop their papers. Would you mind giving her a hand? It's just for this period. Downstairs, room 3A.'

Cassie looked shocked. There was something decidedly odd about this — but being asked to help teach another class was a temptation that Cassie couldn't possibly pass up. When she was gone, Brother Frank shut the door.

'New uniform?' he asked.

'I just think this is more flattering,' I said.

He didn't laugh. This was troubling.

'Your friend Allison,' he said. 'How is she?'

'She'll be okay,' I said. 'Someday.'

He nodded.

'That was very unfortunate. I'm sure she's upset. I've never taught her. I take it math isn't her strong suit?'

'She doesn't really have a strong suit,' I said honestly. 'She's kind of, you know.'

'A normal student,' he said. 'Unlike you.'

It had never been said so bluntly.

'Let's not dance around the subject, Jane,' he said. 'You're not a normal student. You don't have a normal mind. You have an exceptional one. This class, for instance. I've had to pace it for Cassie, and I think I might kill her as it is. We're about to enter some topics in abstract algebra, which, to be perfectly honest, are never, ever attempted on a high school level. This is what I teach my second years at MIT.'

I felt my cheeks glow a little. Praise from Brother Frank actually meant something. It was nice to be having this cozy little moment together on this otherwise tragic day. Maybe he knew I needed a pick-me-up.

'We need to talk, Jane,' he said. 'That's why I asked Cassie to leave.'

'About what?'

'About what it means to be here, at St. Teresa's,' he said. 'It would be unfortunate if the only developments you made here were academic. We need to talk about how you're going to apply your talents to this world. I know that you don't believe in everything this school stands for and teaches...'

'Are you talking about religion class?' I asked. 'Okay. I debate with Mr. Jenkle every once in a while.'

'According to the guidance report, you called him a crypto-fascist during a discussion on reproductive rights in class yesterday.'

'Well,' I said, looking up at the ceiling. 'Yeah, I kind of did that.'

'Look, Jane,' he said. 'I happen to agree with you on many of those issues, but that isn't the point. The point *is*, Jane...'

He started turning his coffee cup slowly. This was not a good sign.

'...The point *is*, Jane...'

A repeat. Really not a good sign.

'...I'm not the only person who keeps track of your behavior.'

'You're saying I'm getting a reputation?'

'You almost have your own file drawer in the guidance office. I don't want to dredge up the past, but it's starting to catch up with you. Your application to a men's seminary school to become a priest. Passing out condoms on Valentine's Day. And look at yourself now.'

I looked down at my very white, very untanned thighs, well exposed by my shorts.

'These are the things people just might remember when you ask them to write your college recommendations in the next few weeks, if you don't do something to repair your image.'

'What are they going to do?' I asked. 'Kick me out? My grades are perfect.'

'But your attitude is not. And there are people who would like to make an example of you. They could kick you out — or they could try to keep you another year. And believe me, though I love you dearly and can barely stand the thought of parting from you, I do not want to see that happen.'

This was sobering news.

'They wouldn't,' I said. 'It's senior year! And I raised the SAT average for the whole school by about sixty points!'

He leaned back and adjusted his stack of *Modern Mathematics* magazines until it was *just so*.

'Jane,' he said slowly. 'I need to ask you something. What do you believe in?'

'What do you mean?'

'I mean, what matters to you? I know you have problems with some of the rules of the Catholic faith, but you must believe in something. What's important to you? What's true? What would you fight for?'

'I fight about a lot of things,' I answered honestly.

'True. But some battles are more important than others.'

I had come into class expecting to answer calculus questions, not explain the state of my eternal soul.

'I guess knowledge,' I said. 'Knowledge matters. I get annoyed when people get things wrong.'

'There are limits to knowledge, Jane. There are greater things in this world.'

'Such as?'

'Such as love,' he said.

'Not interested,' I said.

'Jane,' he said. 'This is going to be hard for you to understand, but this is going to be a difficult year. It will not be like the other years.'

'I know. Senior year. Adulthood, responsibility, the fate of the world on our young shoulders...'

'This is no joke, Jane.' He sounded more grave than I'd ever heard him. 'You have to realize something. You have gifts. You are exceedingly blessed with intelligence. But you lack willpower. You are often lazy and combative.'

I looked down modestly. Such flattery.

'I don't say that to be critical,' he went on. 'The academic world is littered with smart people who are lazy and combative. They are lazy because they have never had to make a lot of effort to keep themselves employed. Just ask your father about those people. And they're naturally arrogant because they think they're better than other people. Trust me. They are not. The best thinkers — the *smartest* people — are the ones who really value other people, value ideas, and work from their hearts. This is something I really think you need to know. And now that I have given what amounts to an Oscar speech...'

He paused and rubbed his bushy brows.

'Jane,' he said. 'Be a good girl this year. For my sake, if not your own.'

I wasn't sure how my friend throwing up somehow

became a reason to lecture me on my behavior. If it had been anyone else but Brother Frank, I would have said something back. But I let him get away with things that others couldn't.

'Okay,' I said. 'For you.'

'Thank you, Jane. It means more to me than you can imagine. And now, do me a favor and go put your uniform back on. You look ridiculous.'

Chapter 6

I'd noticed a long time ago that A3 seemed to have entirely different biological needs. They were all really dry and doing things that seemed like things you do to your exotic lizard, not to your human self. They were huge on lotions, balms, glosses, Vaseline... you name it.

Elsie always carried a small aerosol can of French spring water with her to spray on the undersides of her wrists. I once spotted her in the second-floor bathroom between classes rubbing her knees with vitamin E oil. Lai was always putting drops in her eyes, the theory being that she needed to after clubbing in Boston all night. Maybe the weirdest — and boldest — was Tracey Pils, who was seen on numerous occasions putting Preparation H under her eyes. I have heard that professional models and pageant contestants do this because PH is the best anti-inflammatory on the market. And I think Tracey was a pageant person once. But still. It takes a certain amount of confidence to be seen doing that.

Being lizard-like, they were perfectly suited to this

lung-deflating heat. I passed them on the way out the door after school, sitting all in a row on a concrete bench, passing around a tube of shea butter.

'Hey, Jane,' Tracey said as I passed. 'Come here a second.'

I don't like being ordered around, but I also didn't feel like causing a scene by ignoring them and walking past. I compromised by stopping and moving a step or two closer so that I was within earshot but hadn't actually gone all the way over to where they were sitting.

'How's Allison?' she asked. 'We heard she was sick earlier.'

It was said innocently. There was barely a trace of malice in that stone-white, heart-shaped face of hers. But just that they were asking was enough. The temptation to say something to her that would send her groveling back to the sinkhole she had obviously crawled out of was strong, but I remembered my lecture from earlier in the day. I needed to be moderate. My attacking Tracey wouldn't help Ally.

'Recovering,' I said, as breezily as I could.

'Guess she didn't manage to get a little, then?'

'Yes, she did.'

That wasn't me who said that. The voice came from behind me. The lanky sophomore from the bathroom trailed up, thin and long as a shadow. Lanalee hooked around in front of me and squared off in front of the A3. Her rust-colored hair was hanging long and free now, all the way down her back. She reminded me of one of those

Renaissance women who got locked up in towers and had to let guys climb up their hair to rescue them.

'I'm her little,' she said. As she spoke, she was casually unwrapping a Twinkie. She consumed this in three easy bites, snapping the golden crumbs off her fingers.

'Who are *you*?' Elise said, taking in Lanalee in a long and totally undisguised up-and-down glance.

'Lanalee Tremone. I just transferred her from Bobbin.'

All three of them looked surprised at that one. Bobbin was the best school in the area. It had the highest population of celebrities' kids anywhere outside of New York or LA, and it was famous for its 'make your own curriculum' police. Bobbin students started their own businesses or went to live on goat farm communes in France or staged massive art installations where they all got naked and painted each other's bodies with condiments. It was about as different from St. Teresa's Preparatory School for Girls as it was possible to get. Going to Bobbin instantly made you interesting.

'Why are you here if you went to *Bobbin*?' Tracey asked.

'I got into a little trouble there. My great-grandparents thought I needed a *more structured environment*, and they were paying the bill.'

This caused a bit of visible doubt in their eyes.

'What house did you live in at Bobbin?' Lai asked.

'Walker.'

'Walker? I partied at Walker!' Lai leaned forward. 'Do you know Paul Weller?'

'Tall Paul? Yeah. He lived in the room on the corner.'

'You know Alex Rye?' Lai asked, her eyebrow arching.

'Rye? He ended up blowing the door off of his room last year doing a *science experiment* of a very illegal nature.'

'Allesandra Fuller?'

'Look, do you want to borrow my Facebook so you can look these people up?' Lanalee said. 'I'm not sure *you* actually know them. And no one parties at Walker anyway. We went to Hepp House for that. I don't know what you were doing, but I doubt it was very interesting.'

A cool silence now. It was time for the A3 to reload and fire, and they clearly had nothing.

'Let's go,' Lanalee said to me. 'I'm getting bored. I need more sugar.'

It was a beautiful performance — I had to give that to her completely.

'How irritating were they?' Lanalee asked when we had turned the corner of the building. 'I hate people who always have to ask if you know people. Who cares if I knew them?'

'Well, they still sound cool,' I said. 'It sounds like those are people to know. There's no one to know here. This school is not a magnet for the to-know people.'

'Trust me, Bobbin's just full of rich freaks. It's not that exciting.'

'Still,' I said, 'it's kind of an accomplishment to get kicked out.'

'I know,' Lanalee said with a long smile. She had very thin lips, but they went on forever. 'That's why I made it up.'

'You were lying?'

'The part about my double Gs was true,' she said. 'They thought this place would be better for me. The school didn't want me because I applied too late, but the GGs are buying the school a new driveway if I can stay.'

We were standing in the driveway by this point. It did kind of look like testing ground for land mines. Lanalee looked out beyond the soccer fields and over to the golden brick mansion opposite us. It was like looking out to Oz. The grass was, quite literally, greener there — because they *had* grass in the places that we had asphalt. Some guys were stretched out on this grass. Other guys were lounging on the long marble steps that led up to the front door or were squatting on the veranda and the various urns and bits of statuary, bouncing soccer balls off each other's heads and snorting.

'That's the guys' school over there, right?' she asked.

'That's St. Sebastian's.'

'It's so much nicer than our school.'

'Trust me,' I said. 'I know. I've been talking about this for three years. It's some old mansion that the church bought. It came with all of this ground, so they built our school over on this side.'

'But why do the guys get that gorgeous place and we get this thing that looks like a bunker?'

'Parking lot,' I corrected her. 'Our school was designed by a guy who was famous for making multi-story parking lots. He just made rooms where the parking spaces used to be and made staircases instead of ramps. I'm not kidding.'

I wasn't either. My dad knew the guy. He taught architecture at Brown, until they realized how awful all of his buildings were.

'This place is just confused,' she said. 'They put guys in the nice building. Why? Guys ruin stuff. And then they separate us with this...'

She lost her words and waved at the eight-foot cyclone fence that separated our soccer fields.

'It gives the place that prison-camp feel,' I said. 'It's nice. I heard they were actually going to put razor wire on top, but it was against some kind of law.'

'I'm not going to be able to handle this,' Lanalee said, her long face drooping.

'Well,' I said, 'if you went to Bobbin, it might be hard to get used to. But it's survivable.'

She bit her lip for a moment.

'Hey,' she said, yanking a rose-stone school ring of her long, pale hand, 'before I forget, can you give this to Allison? I haven't been able to find her.'

I put it on my thumb. For a moment, I wished this girl could have been my little. I wanted to steal her... but then I felt bad. No matter what, Ally had had a much worse day than I had. She deserved Lanalee.

'Can I ask you something?' she said. 'That story on the Junior Judges page about Allison. Something about the prom. What was that all about?'

'Ally just had a bad experience,' I said, twisting the ring down to try to keep it on my finger.

'What happened?'

'She met a guy,' I said. 'It didn't work out. She was really upset.'

This was really a mild retelling — like saying that the sinking of the *Titanic* was a little problem with a boat on a cold night.

'There's more to it than that,' Lanalee said. 'Isn't there? You can tell me. I like her. I just don't want to say the wrong thing, you know?'

She cocked her head in a curious manner. I hesitated. I hated this story, but Lanalee had proven herself, both my signing on with Ally and by taking on the A3. She had earned the right to know.

'Okay,' I said, lowering my voice. 'It's not a secret, but she doesn't like talking about it, so don't bring it up, okay?'

'Understood,' she said.

'Ally really wanted to go to the prom last year,' I said. 'School events mean a lot to her. But she had no one to ask.'

'But there's a school full of guys right there,' Lanalee said, pointing.

'They don't let us mix much here at the gulag,' I explained. 'And Ally sometimes finds it hard to meet people in person. So, she went online, to some Boston teen dating site.'

'Ah,' she said knowingly. 'E-love.'

'She met this guy who called himself Hawkster...'

'Hawkster?'

'I know. She got kind of... obsessed. I kept trying to

warn her about getting too crazy about someone she didn't know, but she didn't want to hear that.'

'What about this countdown?' Lanalee asked.

'She started doing this countdown thing, ticking off each week, day, minute, hour, and second to anyone who said hello to her. She texted me at random points to give me the count. She left notes in my locker with times on them and nothing else. One time she wrote "5 d, 6 h, 37 m, 14 s" on the back of my hand. But it was cute — she's not crazy.'

'Okay,' Lanalee said with a nod. 'She was a little wound up. It happens. I'm with you.'

And she *was* with me. Her face was intent, studious.

'The thing is,' I went on, 'they made this deal that they wouldn't exchange pictures, or even real names, until a few hours before. Al got all dressed up, had her hair done, everything. She sent off her picture... and the guy went silent. She thought maybe he'd left his house already, so she went to the prom and waited. All night she checked her cell phone. She called me at home to have me check her e-mail.'

'You were at home?'

'My boyfriend and I had just broken up,' I said, waving my hand. 'We weren't planning on going anyway. The point is, web guy went subsonic. Dead. She waited for three hours before she gave up and called me to go and get her.'

'Oh, wow,' Lanalee said. 'That sucks. Did she ever hear from him?'

'No,' I said. 'She never did. She never really got over

it. She always thought it was her picture. It made her hate the way she looks.'

A black Lincoln Town Car sidled up the drive, carefully plodding its way among the holes.

'That's my ride,' she said. 'Take this.'

She reached into her bag and pulled out a small lavender card with her name, address, and phone number printed in dark purple script.

'My grandmother always gets me these things,' she said. 'They're supposed to be for events, *society* things. Don't laugh. They're great to take to parties. Really.'

I wasn't laughing. I was feeling the heavy, fine card stock. It had a rosy scent. This kind of little touch, combined with the Bobbin and the driveway stories, meant that Lanalee came from one of *those* families. Those families that went sailing off Newport at spring break, who had friends who lived in brownstones or mansions in Federal Hill, and had Uncle So-and-so's old Yale sweater in the trunk of the car, just in case they needed an extra layer when they went skiing.

'Have to go,' she said, loping to the car. 'But I've decided. Allison will be my project for the year. I need one, or I'm not going to be able to cope. We'll make it right.'

This was all rattled off in one breath and punctuated by the muffled slamming of the car door. The car remained still for a moment, then a loud burst of opera rumbled from within. Whoever was driving hit the gas, sending the massive car off on a kind of extreme rally drive, almost taking out Sister Philmonilla as she watered the flowers at the base of the statue of St. Teresa. Sister put her hand to her heart to steady herself and looked at me disapprovingly. I knew she was about to come over and lecture me on safe driving, even though I had nothing to do with it, so I pretended not to see her and quickly turned and jogged down the driveway.

Chapter 7

You know how in those really tiny countries — the ones with a population of two people and three pounds of assorted fruit — the leaders always wear big hats and huge aviator sunglasses? It happens in nature too. Animals puff up to make themselves look bigger. Cats do it. Owls do it. It's the *puffing instinct*. Rhode Island puffs. Rhode Island isn't actually called Rhode Island — the real name is the State of Rhode Island and Providence Plantations. We don't use it because it takes up more space than we have. We're small. Vermont is a superpower compared to us. If you screw up in Rhode Island, the news goes statewide in about ten minutes. There is no escape.

And we have trolleys in Providence. That's how we get around if we don't drive. It was no shock that I found Allison waiting for the trolley or that I found most of our school waiting with her. In fact, it seemed like half of Rhode Island was waiting for our trolley.

Allison barely turned as I approached. It wasn't cold. She just looked like she wanted to be unrecognizable. I think she would have gladly erased her entire existence and embraced that happy state of nonbeing that Eastern religions are always talking about. I stood by her silently. Unfortunately, my joining her only drew attention. A clump of weedy Sebastian's guys started chin-upping in interest.

'Hey, barf bag,' one of them said.

I fixed my eye on him.

'Ignore him, Jane,' Allison said.

'But Al…'

'Let me handle it myself, okay?'

I let that go for her sake, but I couldn't do the same for the giggling sophomore who was staring Ally up and down but pretending to be fascinated by her phone.

'Haven't you ever seen one of those magical talking calculators before, sweetheart?' I said innocently.

The girl's eyes went wide. I felt Ally's elbow land softly in my ribs.

'Sorry,' I said.

'Forget it,' she said. 'I'm going for a walk.'

I started to go with her, but she indicated with a shake of the head that she wanted to go home alone. It was hard to let her go, but I could see she meant it. Many eyes followed her as she walked off.

Three zip codes' worth of people tried to get onto the trolley when it came, meaning that we were all squashed together. I managed to take advantage of my height and wriggle through to an open spot under a handle bar. Out of the corner of my eye, I saw someone giving up their seat to a girl with a cast on her arm who couldn't hold on. I could only see his back, but I knew from the gesture and from the exact length of the back, the way the gray Sebastian's shirt just came out of the top of his pants over on the left, it could only be Elton.

Like I said, it had been six months, three weeks, and two days — the healing process was well under way. But still, what exactly are you supposed to do when the only decent, the only truly intelligent, the only really perfect guy within the entire metropolitan area dumps you for no reason at all? If you are me, you curl up in a ball for two weeks and refuse to eat, then you do things like apply to a men's seminary school, pass out condoms at your Catholic school, argue with teachers, get a small tattoo, and stop doing homework. You go through that phase for about two months. And from that point on, you just overeat and generally lose control of your own mind whenever you see your ex. This plan had been working like a charm for me so far.

I tried to turn and get off, but I was wedged in. I almost knocked a baby out of her mother's grip in the effort. The trolley doors shut and bang — Elton and I were two feet from each other, separated only by a slightly smelly guy who looked like he was probably from the art school. (He was wearing a big striped scarf. Only an artist guy wouldn't change his look on a ninety-five-degree day.)

This was the closest I had gotten to Elton all this school year. He still had a tan. He had stopped spiking up his hair in the middle. It was longer now, a bit more romantic and shaggy, sweeping over the tops of his round glasses. I could see the pattern of his T-shirt through his white Sebastian's dress shirt — it was his 'Geek' shirt. I had gotten him that shirt last Christmas, back when I had no hint at all that things would soon blow up and change.

'Hey, Jane,' he said. But it wasn't a friendly 'Hey, Jane.' It was a 'You are staring at the spot where my heart is located with an intensity that unnerves me' kind of 'Hey, Jane.'

'Oh, hi,' I said. Though there was no way he would ever believe I hadn't noticed him, I still tried to pretend like I hadn't. I stared at the art school guy's book (it was called *The Waye of the Witch*, if you're interested) until he saw this and turned away.

In my mind, I said the best things to Elton. I wrote countless excellent notes that I never sent. I came up with clever and highly detailed imaginary situations in which we were thrown together and somehow made him realize that life without me was a hollow shell. but he didn't look like a hollow shell. He looked like he was back on the soccer team, all calf muscles and lean body. He looked sane and full of life. He was not, as I had hoped, pale, consumptive, and constantly weeping and mumbling my name.

And neither was I. Not anymore. But none of those wonderful things I had scripted out came to mind. Instead, what I blurted was, 'Allison puked today.'

'I heard,' he said. And because he was Elton and not an ordinary, snorting Sebastianite, he seemed genuinely concerned. 'Hope she's okay.'

I nodded and found myself staring at the floor, unable to continue the conversation. I tried. I searched every part of my brain for something to say, but it was an empty vault. So I took the easy route out — I excused myself and got off at the next stop, then walked a mile home.

It was, in short, a terrible day. But it was behind me.

Chapter 8

Here, for your edification, is Jane's first law of lateness. Given that

a. you don't fall asleep until 3 a.m. because you sit up all night writing e-mails to your ex-boyfriend that you are never going to send,
b. your power goes out somewhere around four in the morning because of freak wind and rainstorm,
c. your obnoxiously loud green alarm clock doesn't go off because you haven't changed the backup battery since you got it (Christmas, age twelve), and
d. you wake up with a sudden start and a horrible feeling in your stomach because you haven't been blasted halfway across the room by the screaming antics of Boston's most annoying morning DJ (station chosen expressly for this purpose),...
the time will be exactly (and I do mean exactly) four minutes before you have to leave for school.

Why four? Partially because five minutes is an accepted unit of time. Four minutes is *just short* of an accepted unit of time. But because you technically have *some* time because you aren't late *yet*, you think you can use that time and do all the things you normally do... just a little more quickly, with the fine points ignored. But the truth is, you just make yourself later in the process.

Joan was in the shower, so I made a pathetic attempt at washing myself up with peach-scented dish soap at the kitchen sink. I evaded any questions from my father, who was standing at the counter slicing a pile of grapefruit. I was still ten minutes late in leaving. I forgot my keys in the process.

The weather was foul. It was pouring down rain. The trolleys were a mess, so I tried to walk. The wind blew my umbrella upside down halfway to school, and I couldn't really get it to turn the right way again. And as a final gesture, I was so busy running up the school driveway that I didn't even try to avoid the countless holes that I couldn't see because they had filled with water. I went right into one, soaking one foot completely and banging up both my knees. Sister Rose Marie passed me a demerit in the lobby for 'throwing open the door with excessive force.'

I checked in at the front office with Sister Mary Bernadette, the principal's secretary. Everyone loved Sister Bernie. She was a tiny slip of a woman, probably ninety years old, with a high, cheerful voice. One of the few blessings in the school was that if you were late, you checked in with Sister Bernie, who had endless sympathy for any story and believed that everyone told the truth. I once tested this famously boundless faith sophomore year, when I overslept. I came in and told Sister Bernie that a pack of dogs got loose from a dog walker and pinned me in between some Dumpsters for half an hour. Sister nodded sadly and patted my hand and said, 'Poor dear. Dogs can be so unpredictable. Mother Mary was with you, though, and kept you safe. No demerits. And stop down in the cafeteria and have something to eat to calm your nerves.'

Needless to say, I felt like such an evil heel after that, I brought Sister a bag of assorted chocolates on Christmas and her feast day every year from that point on. And I still couldn't look her in the eye.

Today I just told her the truth. She gave me some tissues to help me dry off and let me go with no more demerits. There is mercy in this world.

I walked down the hall as silently as I could, considering that my school shoes were squeaking. It always gave me a very bad feeling walking around between classes. When the halls weren't filled with other people and movement and noise, that's when I noticed all the statues. I think we had more statues than the Louvre. But they weren't statues you would want to find peeking out at you from a dark corner. They were all either clumsy ceramic renderings that managed to make saints look like rejected characters from *Star Wars*, or they were highly detailed, highly accurate images of saints in intense pain, like the one at the end of the hallway I was in — the one that showed you, in graphic detail, St. Sebastian as he was struck by a dozen arrows at once.

I rounded the corner and found myself facing an entire wall of flyers. These flyers weren't on the bulletin boards, which in itself was a shock. We were only allowed to use bulletin boards for flyers, and then only for official school club announcements. Someone had actually had the guts to plaster an actual wall with their own flyers. And they were all exactly the same, containing only one sentence. They read: WILL YOU BE ASKED?

I followed the line of flyers with amazement. There was no way that anyone would have been able to do this without being noticed. I instinctively sped up. I didn't want to be seen anywhere near these flyers, not with my recent warnings. They wouldn't have even liked it if I was tacking up signs that said: SEX SUX! GIRLS' SCHOOL RULES!

The door to English was closed, of course. The period had started fifteen minutes before, which was well beyond the point of recovery. Our school hated lateness in general, but Sister Charles hated it in a very particular sort of way, like we were deliberately stealing time from her life and she planned on extracting it back from us somehow.

As I opened the door, I heard her saying, 'The overall poor quality of the last batch of essays you turned in makes me wonder if any of you know how to read, much less write...'

She trailed off as she noticed me. I waited for the blow, but she switched her focus and continued as if I wasn't even there.

'So,' she went on. 'We will return to basics, as you do with children. An essay takes a stand. It presents an opinion. I may be assuming too much, but I think you all have opinions.'

I sidestepped as gingerly as I could between desks and made it to my own. I had never noticed before how loud this was — the deafening rip of my zipper, the unbearable scratching sound of pages being turned. The fact that Sister chose to ignore me was about ten times worse than getting chewed out. It seemed to suggest that she was waiting to unleash something truly unholy on me at any moment.

Out of the corner of my eye, I saw that there was a strange girl at Allison's desk. My brain played a bit of a trick on me because though I could see the girl was in a St. Teresa's uniform, I first assumed she was a visiting student, sitting in on a class. Over the next few seconds, my brain re-scanned the image and told me something stranger.

That girl was Allison. In a wig.

At least, my brain said, that's what it had to be because whatever was on her head was not the Ally fro I knew and loved. Instead of her somewhat washy red blond, her hair was a blitz of cascading deep red, with a blond streak coming right out of the front. Plus, most of it was gone. It had been chopped into a pert little bob, right at the point where her hair usually bent and started to look awkward. Now it looked like a little red helmet.

It was adorable. It even made her forehead look perfectly proportioned.

'Miss Jarvis,' Sister said, 'as you've developed a very becoming slack jaw, perhaps you'd like to tell us about the kinds of rhetorical appeals that we may utilize in composition?'

I searched around in my head for an answer, but a tiny red-helmeted cartoon figure of Allison was running around, scrambling the normally well-ordered facts.

'There are three basic kinds of appeals,' I said. 'There's...'

All I could think about was that shiny red bob.

'... logos. That's the appeal to...'

The shiny redness of it. That was my best friend's *head*. The head of the girl who had had the exact same hairstyle since the sixth grade. A kind of... lumpy thing.

'...reason. There's also...'

Nothing. White noise. I looked at Sister, but her image was hazy to me. My face fell soft and dumb and blank.

'I see,' she said. 'The great Miss Jarvis does not know. Are you too warm, Miss Jarvis?'

I didn't reply. Sister shifted her gaze to Allison.

'Miss Concord,' she said. 'I see you have recovered. And it looks like you've spent the evening at the hairdresser. I think you might have spent it better sitting at home and reading your book. But perhaps you can contribute something to this conversation?'

The voice that came from the redheaded girl was calm and clear, not the dry stuttering that was so soothing and familiar.

'There's also pathos,' it said. 'The appeal to emotion, and ethos, which is when you try to convince the audience that they should listen to you because you have a good character and you are knowledgeable.'

Sister stood very still and took a good look at Allison. It seemed like she was seeing her for the first time.

'Oh?' she said. 'This is certainly interesting. Can you elaborate?'

'Well, Sister,' Allison said, 'Cicero, maybe the most famous of Roman orators, said the last method, ethos, is really kind of conceited, but it works. He used it a lot himself. He felt that it should only be used in the exordium, the introduction.'

This was enough of an unusual occurrence to get the attention of everyone in the room. They were all looking at Allison now.

'Could it be,' Sister said, 'that a St. Teresa's girl had actually read her book and taken note of its contents? My prayers have not gone unanswered.'

I didn't have to turn and look to know that the redheaded girl smiled. I could feel it in my spine.

I cornered Ally the second the bell rang.

'Your hair,' I said. 'What did you *do* to it?'

She reached up and touched her head gently, as if she was petting a baby bunny I had just informed her was squatting there.

'I just decided I needed a change,' she said. 'So I went out last night and got my hair done. Do you like it?'

'It's nice,' I said uncertainly. 'I'm just getting used to it. I wish you had told me.'

'I don't actually need permission from you to get my hair done,' she snapped.

Ally had never snapped at me before.

'I didn't say that,' I said. 'I was just worried.'

'I think you're pissed off that I knew something you didn't,' she said. 'Feeling stupid sucks, huh?'

And with that, she walked away.

I'd never argued with Allison before. Allison was my best friend. A fight between us was so unfamiliar and unexpected — something unthinkable, like someone in their first earthquake, unable to accept the fact that the earth is wiggling like jelly under their feet. Literally. I felt a little unsteady as I went down the hall.

That's when I noticed that all of those flyers were gone. Not even a piece of tape remained to show where they had been.

Chapter 9

At the end of the day, all I really wanted to do was go home. I still had no keys, though. That meant I had to go all the way across town to The Pink Peppercorn to borrow my mom's. I snagged a chunk of apricot cheesecake on the way out and ate it with my fingers right out of the bag.

As I was leaving, a little sports car approached. It was small and tight in an autobahn-ready kind of way and was a steely shade of silver. The back of it was swollen and curvy, and the front was very small, with the two front wheels set off from the body of the car. It pulled along the curb. A man in a very neat pin-striped suit stepped out and came over to the menu case, near where I was standing with my hand in a gloopy mess of cheesecake.

'Can you tell me,' he said, 'what time this restaurant opens? I have heard some very good things about it.'

'I think... five, maybe?' I said.

'Don't you work here?'

'No.'

He stepped back and looked me up and down, then nodded in satisfaction.

'That is a school uniform you're wearing,' he said. 'Not the uniform of a waitress. My apologies.'

'Don't worry about it. But it is a good restaurant. My mom works here.'

'*Does* she?' He seemed delighted by this. He leaned over me to examine the menu in its little glass box, mumbling some appreciation under his breath.

'A pumpkin risotto. How apropos for this time of year. And a lovely lamb chop with sauté of baby vegetables. Oh yes. Delectable. I do like my food *young*. But what would *you* recommend?'

This was unpleasant and affected but not entirely unexpected. Providence does attract a lot of freaky foodies.

'The squid's good,' I said. 'They stuff it with fennel. Or something.'

'Ah. Calamari. Yes. Yes, yes, yes.'

A dog's black muzzle popped out of the car window and sniffed at the air eagerly.

'Providence is a fine town for dining,' the man went on, tapping on the glass with his finger. 'I think it rivals New York. And so many fine houses. Many of the lovely houses in this town...'

He stopped tapping and swung his gaze up suddenly.

'Do you know what paid for many of them?' he asked.

I remained silent, like you're supposed to do when someone wants to impress you with something they know.

'Slavery,' he said, grinning slowly, revealing a mouth

full of small, delicate teeth. 'Strange how there's a dark underbelly to so many beautiful things.'

'There's a lot of ugly history,' I said. 'I guess every place has a hidden story.'

'That is absolutely true,' he said. Something in my answer seemed to have pleased him because he extended his hand in a very businesslike fashion. I'm not used to getting handshakes, so I took it uncertainly. His hand was freezing, and his skin was almost gray, but his nails were better manicured than mine (meaning, they were manicured) and his grip was firm. If he noticed the traces of cheesecake on my fingers, he didn't show it.

'My name is Mr. Fields, by the way. And what is yours, young lady?'

'Jane,' I said.

'An excellent, simple name but one of greatness! And certainly one with history. There was a queen of England named Jane. She was queen for nine days.'

'Jane Grey,' I said. 'I know. I was named for her.'

This was true. I was named for Jane Grey, and my sister was named for Joan of Arc. Both great women of history — both met very bad ends. I don't know what my parents were trying to tell us with that one.

'This interests me very much,' Mr. Fields said, pulling a pair of round glasses from his breast pocket and putting them on hastily to examine me more closely. 'You were named for her, you say?'

I nodded.

'You must be an exceptional young lady,' he said. 'I can see that. Lady Jane Grey — she too was an exceptional young lady. Fifteen years old and nine days of total power before they beheaded her.'

He seemed to be drawing a line with his eyes across my neck. I pulled up the collar of my coat.

'It was a pleasure speaking to you, Jane,' he said. 'We will return at five to enjoy some lamb chops, which I am certain will be excellent. Have a very good day.'

He walked back to his car and drove off. He slowly wove away, leaving me to wonder about the general weirdness that was following me. There was something wrong in Providence today, and I, for one, was going home to hide from it.

Chapter 10

On the trolley home, I tried to read our English assignment, the first two chapters of *Moby Dick*. It was a fish book. I wasn't feeling it. I took out a vampire novel called *Fondled by Shadows* that Ally had given me a few weeks before and tried to lose myself in that. Vampires had never done much for me, but Ally loved them. (Basically, if it had a witch or a vampire in it, Ally was there.) I tried as hard as I could, but I bailed at the first glint of pointy teeth and shoved it back into my bag.

I looked out of the window to see that the sky had gone from gray to a kind of milky green, and it had begun to move, like it was being slowly stirred by a great celestial spoon. The heat that had crushed us the entire day lifted all at once, and by the time I got off, there was a decidedly cool edge to the air. Weather, I knew, was not supposed to change that quickly — and if it did, something was about to happen. I had several blocks before I would be home, and I wanted to make it.

As I exited the trolley, I felt a sharp sting on the soft,

very think skin just under my right eye. It felt exactly like the time Allison accidentally pennied me in the face when we were sophomores. I wiped it off my face. It was a tiny piece of ice.

'Not good,' I said to myself, speeding up.

Something landed by my feet — something that looked like a small Ping-Pong ball but was also a piece of ice. I heard a *clunk*. A car alarm behind me went off. Another clunk came from next to me. An ice ball bounced heavily off the hood of a car. The sound of ice hitting metal and the echo of car alarms ran the entire length of the street.

I broke into a full run and the pelting really began. A chunk of ice punched right through someone's mailbox like it was made of paper. My legs were pumping harder than I'd ever forced them to go. I heard a windshield break at the same time I felt something like a baseball hit my ankle and I went down in the street.

'Move, Jane,' I told myself as I got to my feet. Ice clipped my ear, my left hand. I was hobbling, and I wasn't sure where to go. There was ice smacking down all around, golf-ball-sized and getting bigger.

Suddenly, an arm was scooping me up and hustling me along. I glanced over at its owner, a tall, young-looking guy.

'Over there,' he said, dragging me in the direction of a large blue house with a full wraparound porch. We literally threw ourselves up its steps and under its overhang.

I took a closer look at the guy who had just plucked me from the street. He was a very reedy Sebastian's student. His uniform was grossly oversized, cinched together by a belt. He had slightly shaggy light red hair and a very finely featured face, with a tiny nose and thin, peaked eyebrows.

'I don't know about this porch roof,' he said, looking up at the beams overhead. The volley of ice struck our shelter with such force that it was hard to hear him speak. I had to move closer.

'Well,' I said, 'I don't think we have much choice. It's not like we can rebuild it right now.'

'No,' he said thoughtfully, as if this had been a serious proposition.

The rain gutter came down with a deafening clang, spearing a shrub like a big white toothpick through a cocktail olive.

'You should get your weight off that ankle,' he said. 'Sit down.'

He helped me onto a rocking chair. I pushed down my sock and examined the fist-sized blue mark that was blossoming there. It immediately overshadowed the marks I'd gotten on my knees that morning.

'I bet that hurts,' he said, squatting to have a good look. 'But it's probably not broken.'

I realized I hadn't had a chance to shave my legs that morning and pulled the sock up.

'It's fine,' I said. 'I'm Jane, by the way.'

'I'm Owen.'

'So, you're a freshman at Sebastian's?'

'Yeah. How did you know?'

'Your uniform,' I said. 'It has the freshman look. It's too big.'

I didn't mean anything by it, but he pulled self-consciously at his shirt. I forget that guys also care about what their clothes look like.

A small black cat scrambled up onto the porch and joined us. As soon as it had reached safety, it started meowing plaintively and ran to me as if it knew me. It wanted to rub against my ankle, but it was too sore. Owen found a plastic bag in his backpack and made me an impromptu ice pack, then he patrolled the edge of the porch, watching the progress of the storm.

'So how do you like Sebastian's?' I asked.

'All high schools are the same,' he said. 'I guess it's kind of easier having all guys. It keeps you focused.'

This was not the point of view of the average freshman Sebastianite. When not snorting, bouncing soccer balls off their heads, or destroying the mansion they occupied, they were up to other equally high-minded pursuits. These ranged from becoming acolytes just so they could hang out in our chapel, to clinging to the fence after school and shouting things like, 'I like your bra. Can I see it?'

'That's one way of looking at it,' I said.

'Yeah.' He shook his head. 'I know. People tell me all the time that I'm too serious.'

We settled into a comfortable silence as we waited out the storm. After about fifteen minutes, it slowed down. The deep green of the sky lifted to a more normal gray, then to sunshine. The ground was thick with ice balls, some smashed to pieces, some still perfectly round. I reached down and picked up one that was easily the size of an orange. People were coming out now, coming into the streets that were completely echoing with car alarms. The sunlight reflected off the ice, nearly blinding us all.

'And they say there's nothing weird happening to the climate,' I said, throwing my ice orange into the ground and smashing it. 'Global warming's a myth.'

'I'll walk you home,' Owen said.

'I'm fine.'

'Just let me,' he said. 'Okay?'

We had to kick our way through the ice at points, but we got back to my house in one piece. My sister was coming up the sidewalk at the same time we were.

'You okay?' she asked. 'This storm was the best!'

Then she noticed Owen. And the fact that I was limping. And that he was supporting me.

One thing I'm pretty certain of: My sister, Joan, will probably not end up on the faculty of MIT. The Nobel Committee will not be calling our house to inform us that she had won a prize. But let me tell you what my sister can do like no one else I've ever known: She can home in on an awkward situation involving me like an awkward-situation-seeking missile. She can read minds and see through walls if something weird is happening to me.

'Don't,' I said.

'What?' she answered.

'I mean it.'

'I'm not!'

She turned to Owen.

'So you are... a guy,' she said.

Owen neither confirmed nor denied. He just blinked at Joan. This conversation was clearly making him nervous.

'I should go,' he said. 'Since we're here. Oh. And here. This is my... e-mail. And phone number. You should call me or something. And can I have yours?'

He produced a pen and a piece of paper. With Joan looking on, I quickly wrote these down.

'Thanks for the help,' I said.

Joan was practically bouncing when he left. She took my bag so that I could hop up the steps to the door. I collapsed onto the sofa and propped up my leg.

'Who's the boyfriend?' she said. 'He had his *arm* around you!'

'The freshman is not my boyfriend.'

'Does that mean you're going to stop obsessing over Elton?'

'I am not obsessed with Elton. I am not anything.'

'Would you say that you have a neuter charge?' she said, clearly trying to show off. 'Like a proton?'

'*Neutral* charge,' I corrected her. 'Protons are positive. Neutrons are neutral. And neuter is what we did to Crick so he wouldn't hump every spaniel in town.'

Crick, our little Scottie, looked up when he heard his name spoken. He looked like a grumpy old man who'd just been disturbed from reading his newspaper.

'Poor widdle wumpkins!' Joan cooed. 'They wook his little noodle! Come here, wumpkins!'

Crick trotted over to Joan merrily, unaware that she had just been casually talking about what had to be one of the most painful and defining moments of his life.

'If you don't want the number,' she went on, 'give it to me. I'll call him.'

'Forget it,' I said, quickly slipping the paper into one of my books.

It wasn't that I didn't like Owen — it was more that I didn't want to get Joan, or anyone else, started on discussions about me or my love life. I had taken a private vow not to even think about that stuff again until I was safely in college.

Thankfully, my father arrived home, and the subject was dropped.

Chapter 11

The TV news trucks rolled into town all through the night. They came from Providence, Boston, New York... they shot from the tops of the highest streets, through broken church windows, did close-ups of the chunks that had been knocked out of the concrete river walk wall.

Our neighborhood had taken a pounding. There were holes punched through our neighbor's car and our shed roof, so we spent the night watching my dad getting bright lights shone in his face while he happily rambled on about velocity and trajectories. (Not that they used any of that stuff in the end. They just said, 'Professor Michael Jarvis of Brown University describes the damage to his property.' And my dad said, 'The ice came through the shed roof.' And that was it. He was very disappointed.)

I developed an ugly green bruise on my ankle but was otherwise okay. I didn't reply to an e-mail that arrived late that night that read:

Really good meeting you. Give me a call, okay?
Owen

~∞~

The first thing we noticed when we got to school the next morning was the statue of St. Teresa that stood by the front door looked like she'd just been in a bar fight and lost. She was pockmarked and blistered, and two of the fingertips at the end of her bashed, outstretched arms had broken off. Eight huge windows at the front of the school had been smashed, and the bevelled glass sign above the door was fragmented into a cloudy mess of filaments held together by nothing but luck, on the verge of blowing into a rain of glass shards.

Inside, things were worse. The fire alarm kept going off. A massive power surge had blown out all the lights, and the hail had broken through a pipe. It was very dark. Water fountains and toilets kept turning themselves on, gushing high, spilling onto the floors. The baffled maintenance men rushed along with Sister Anna Thomas, our hale and hearty head of school. Some tapped on walls and dragged buckets, while the others carried long boxes of fluorescent lightbulbs.

As I was struggling with my lock in the dark, there was an announcement that classes were postponed for an hour and that we were to go and wait in the gym. It was obvious that there was no way they'd be able to enforce this, and everyone seemed to know it. For the first time in my memory, orderly St. Teresa's became a bit of a real free-for-all. It was impossible to really tell who was who, and there was a huge amount of noise as everyone started talking and randomly screaming when they got splashed and the alarms started going again.

In the chaos, I almost didn't notice the large figure of Brother Frank hustling through the dark, guiding Sister Charles in my direction.

'Jane,' he said, clasping me by both shoulders and startling me. 'Quite a storm, that. Last night, eh?'

He was out of breath, for no apparent reason. It wasn't like you walked that fast when you were with Sister Charles. Worry also made him more Irish-sounding.

'Yeah. I got trapped on a porch with a guy.'

'A guy, eh? What guy is this, then?'

'Some freshman from Sebastian's.'

He turned back and glanced at Sister Charles. I could have smacked myself. Everything must seem sexual if you're a nun or a brother.

'It wasn't anything,' I added quickly. 'We just got stuck walking home. It was pretty bad.'

'Right. No. Grand. Grand. Got home safely, then? Quiet night, otherwise?'

He heaved himself against the lockers with a deep puff of breath, as if he liked to have these kinds of casual talks with me every morning. Which he sometimes did, just not in the hall, in the dark, with Sister Charles wobbling next him and the entire school coming down around us.

'Well, yeah. I was, you know, doing homework,' I said.

He seemed to relax now.

'Don't lie to a man of the cloth, Jane,' he said. 'I've

been in this business too long. As long as you're safe. As long as you're safe.'

'Mother Mary was with you,' Sister Charles said sternly, but, to my surprise, with a real sound of relief in her voice. She reached over and put her veiny hand on my arm and gripped it with surprising strength.

'Right,' I said. 'Definitely.'

She withdrew and took hold of Brother Frank's heavy arm, and they continued their slow way through the hall. I managed to get the locker open and was fumbling through it blindly when Allison crept up.

'I've been looking for you,' she said. 'I'm sorry about yesterday. I was just feeling weird.'

'Don't worry about it,' I said.

An announcement came over the intercom saying that they were giving up the effort. The school was too dark and too wet to stay open, and we were all being directed to go home. Buses were coming. Parents were being called.

'Perfect,' I said. 'Let's get out of here. Come to my house with me. We'll feast on leftovers and watch TV until our irises explode!'

Ally hesitated, gripping my locker door for a moment. 'I can't,' she said. 'Maybe later?'

'What do you mean, can't?' I asked. 'It's not like you had other plans. It's a free day.'

'I promised would do something for someone if we closed,' she said, looking down. 'I'm really sorry.'

There was almost no use having a day off with no best friend to spend it with. I slammed my locker door in frustration, thinking that for once, I would not be identified

80

because of the dark and could get away with it. And I did. I stormed off, only to meet up with Sister Rose Marie as I flew through the lobby and got flagged for 'lack of caution in adverse conditions.'

Chapter 12

It's fair to say that up until this point in our history, Allison had been the most predictable person I'd ever known. When she wasn't at school, she was at either one of two places: at home and easy to reach or with me and therefore extremely easy to reach. She didn't go out, except with me. Predictable was good. We were best friends, always together. No secrets. Our lives and schedules were open books.

But after the storm, all of that changed. I had no idea why. For the next week, I only saw Ally in class and maybe a few minutes before or after school. Every night, she had 'something' she had to do. A few times she told me that her mom needed her help or her family was going out. If this was true, the Concords were more active than they had been in the entire time I'd known them. And apparently, they were going shopping because on each day, I noticed Ally had something new. One day, a brown leather jacket. The next, a black-and-silver Coach bag. Then came a silver bracelet, followed by a chunky silver choker to match. Finally, there was a new cell phone that Ally didn't seem to know how to use. Her slim little bag would start to vibrate in class, and she'd smack it desperately, trying to get it to stop. Who was calling her, I had no idea.

When I tried to ask her where these things had come from, she said her aunt Claire had sent them. This was sort of possible — Allison's aunt Claire worked for a multinational bank and made a ton of money. But she was also mean and gave famously cheap Christmas presents, like five-dollar gift cards wrapped up in novelty socks, which Ally would dutifully wear.

Then the week was over. The weekend was a silent one. I sat around, bored and miserable. I convinced Joan that Earth actually had a second moon, which we could never see because it was made of glass, but even that didn't provide much joy. I called Ally, but she never answered, either because she was busy or because she couldn't figure out how to. So I fell back on my standard activity for when I had too much time on my hands — I wrote a six-page note to Elton, which took me four hours and which I promptly destroyed when I was done.

But I wasn't totally forgotten because my e-mail inbox was full of notes from my new friend, Owen. They streamed in, relentless and terse:

Hey, it's Owen. Want to talk?

Haven't heard from you. Want to hang out?

Doing anything today? Call me?

This alarmed me. This was crazy fresh-guy behavior.

When he showed up at our door on Sunday evening, I had Joan send him away. She had to make up a story on the fly, so she told him I was out getting 'a really complicated waxing.'

'Why won't you talk to him?' she asked. 'He's cute.'

'He's a freshman,' I said, moving the dog and throwing myself onto the sofa. 'And he's stalking me.'

'Yeah, but stalking is kind of cool. My friend Kiera got stalked by this guy Ryan. He used to break into her locker and read all of her e-mail, and one time he took her phone and wrote down all the phone numbers. But then they got together, and they've been dating for like a year! Which is kind of creepy, but also really romantic.'

I decided not to comment.

'And he's cute. So cute! He has little vampire eyebrows!'

'Vampire eyebrows?'

'You know how vampires have eyebrows that are pointy like their teeth? It's, like, the teeth point down, and the eyebrows point up? His teeth aren't pointy, though. And vampires are always trying to get into your house. They can't come in unless you ask them...'

She trailed off thoughtfully and jumped when the phone rang. I was wondering why both my sister and my best friend devoted so much thought-time to vampires when the phone landed in my lap.

'No,' I silently mouthed to Joan. 'I'm not home.'

'It's some girl,' she said, waving her hand.

It was Lanalee.

'Get your galoshes on,' she said. 'We're going on a trip!'

'Galoshes?' I repeated. I'd only ever heard my gran use that word.

'Whatever. Allison and I'll be there in ten minutes. Be outside.'

'For what? Allison is with you?'

There was a click.

Chapter 13

‒‒◝◜◞

I'd been used to the steep streets of Providence all my
life, but I'd never experienced taking them on with
Lanalee Tremone tanking around at about eighty miles an
hour in a car the size of a garden shed. The inside was
deeply dark and reeked of clove cigarettes and musky rose.
Lanalee kept fumbling with the radio, blasting a piano
solo that rippled all around the inside of the car.

Allison sat in the front seat with her knees drawn up
to her chest. She had cocooned herself in the snow-white
pom-pom wrap she was wearing, another recent acquisition.
I had the massive backseat all to myself. I couldn't find
the seat belt in the dark, so I kept sliding from door to
door on the slick leather seats. I guessed this was the start
of Lanalee's 'project.'

'You're sixteen?' I asked, clawing for the handle on
the right side door for support.

'Not *exactly*,' Lanalee shouted over the music. 'I can
use the car, though. I've been driving forever. This car is
great. You like Chopin?'

Chopin was deafening us, and we were almost certainly going to kill some other people, so I confined myself to a weak smile.

'I saw it on one of the school blogs,' Lanalee said. 'Some people came in over the weekend for a yearbook meeting. They found it when they were taking some general background shots of the school. They're going to take it down.'

'Saw what? You still haven't told me what we're doing.'

'No time!' She waved her hand at me. 'No time! You'll see.'

When we arrived at the long wooded drive that led to St. Teresa's and St. Sebastian's, Lanalee turned off the headlights and crept along at about ten miles an hour. This felt considerably better speed-wise, but since it was completely black out and we were in a black car with tinted windows, we ran a disproportionately high risk of hitting an animal or, more alarmingly, one of the brothers or sisters walking back home from town. I was going to point this out to Lanalee, but it seemed best not to distract her. I think she managed to hit every single pothole on the way in, which was something of an accomplishment.

We managed to get to the parking lot without killing anything and glided silently past a parked truck from an asphalt company.

'My insurance policy,' Lanalee said, pointing at it.

The school was dark and still, with just a few lights flickering in the windows where repair work was still going on. St. Teresa, still wounded from the storm, looked down on us as we stepped out of the car.

'Hey,' I said to Ally. 'Busy week, huh?'

'Yeah,' she said quietly. 'Sort of.'

'Come on!' Lanalee said, sprinting off toward the building. Ally and I looked at each other, then followed her. Over the doorway, covering up the taped-up bevelled glass sign, was a printed banner made of several pieces of paper taped together. It bore the previous message: WILL YOU BE ASKED?

'Come on,' Lanalee said. 'It's inside.'

'What is?' I asked.

'Come on!'

Lanalee dance-stepped her way into the building. To my surprise, Allison followed her without hesitation. It went against my better judgement, but I trailed right along with them.

Our school could be unnerving at the best of times, but in the dark, it was really odd. The sisters used the cafeteria for their dinner, so the whole place reeked of boiled beef and cabbage. We crept through the lobby, up the stairs, past the office. I decided not to look as we passed the giant oil painting of six medieval nuns being stoned to death for being Catholic and falling into a mass grave. (A nice little calling card they used to terrify incoming students and generally set a happy tone.)

When Lanalee turned the corner to the hall that led to the chapel, I stopped.

'I don't think we should go in there,' I said. 'The sisters use the chapel at night sometimes.'

'We'll be fast,' she said, grabbing me. 'And look!'

Allison was already through the chapel doors, her little red bob swinging with every step.

'This is *good* for her,' Lanalee whispered to me. 'She needs to develop some courage. We'll be in and out.'

'I can't get caught,' I said. '*My* grandparents aren't giving the school a driveway.'

'You won't! Relax!'

Inside, we could immediately see the cause of the commotion. Three grotesque inflatable female mannequins had been lashed to the statues near the altar. They were dressed as nuns, but their mouths were harshly smeared with painful red lipstick. Balanced by their feet was a handwritten sign that read:

THE POODLE CLUB IS HERE AND ANNOUNCES THE SOCIAL EVENT OF THE YEAR: POODLE PROM. WILL YOU BE ASKED?

'That,' Lanalee said with a huge smile, 'is definitely a *message*. It's a strange message, but it's a message.'

I ripped down a flyer and read it over a few times, then looked to Allison. She was strangely still, mesmerized by the sight. There was a noise from above us, which caused us all to jump. It was probably just a tool being dropped, but it still seemed too close.

'Time to go,' Lanalee said.

We slid out of the chapel without any problem, but when we turned the corner, there was a figure between us and the only way out. From the looping walk, it was clearly Sister Charles. She was struggling to get to us. The light in the hall was dim, so though she could see us, she probably was too far to tell who we were.

'Take off your coats,' Lanalee said quietly. 'Quick. And flip them inside out.'

I yanked off my coat and flipped it.

'Over your head,' Lanalee said, draping hers over herself. 'So she can't see who you are. And run.'

'But she's *right there*,' Allison said despairingly.

'What is she going to do? Tackle us? Cover and run!'

Lanalee took off first. There was no time to think this one over. I put my coat over my head, hunkered down, and ran for it. Ally followed.

It was a pathetic sight, really. Sister Charles looked surprised by the three hunching figures coming at her but then squared off resolutely. We were all around her at once; Lanalee went to the left, so she turned that way, but I was on the right. She almost fell over while trying to move herself. She swung out and partially knocked Allison's coat off her, but Lanalee grabbed it and pulled her along.

The run through the rest of the school was like something out of a video game — lots of quick, dodging movement through dark corridors. Then we were outside. We didn't stop running until we got to the car, which slipped off the property probably before Sister Charles could even get to the house phone.

Chapter 14

It was all down the next morning. You would never have known that anything had happened. The school was the same barely lit leaking concrete box that we'd seen the day before, only slightly less treacherous.

But everyone did know — the report had gotten around. You could almost feel the question pulsing through the halls, a kind of physical desperation. What was the Poodle Club? What was this Poodle Prom?

'It's not a sorority,' I heard a junior saying as I came in, 'it's sort of a branch of Skull and Bones, that secret society at Yale that really important people join.'

'Yeah, it's at the other schools,' added a sophomore. 'It's at all the major academies. All the boarding schools. My friend knows someone who goes to Spence in New York, and it's totally there.'

I passed the A3 deep in conference. They were spraying and balming themselves anxiously. Even Cassie was all wound up about it in calculus.

'It's like a secret admissions committee,' she said. 'They get reports back.'

'Who?' I asked.

'The schools!'

'Which schools?'

'I don't know,' she said, shaken. 'But if you're in the Poodle Club, you're in.'

'Who told you this?' I asked.

'Everyone knows,' she said. 'I guess we've finally made it onto their radar. It's probably because of us. You and me.'

Cassie was one of those people, I could tell, who would fall for absolutely everything she heard in college. That story about automatically getting all A's if your roommate dies. Rumors of dorms that had pools on the roof.

There was a squawk, and the intercom came alive.

'Jane Jarvis,' it said, 'please report to Sister Albert's office at once. God bless.'

Cassie gave me a look that said, *See?*

Sister Albert was the principal of our school. She and I had spent some quality time together — and with Brother Frank's warning, I was definitely not happy about being called in.

'What are you here for, dear?' Sister Bernie asked, leaning over her counter. She leaned in close enough that I got a good look at a jagged tear running down the arm of her habit, which she had sewn up in rough, Frankensteiny stitches. This was also the kind of thing that always got to me. It reminded me that the sisters really were poor.

'I don't know,' I lied.

'All right, then,' she said happily. 'Mother Mary be with you, Jane, dear.'

Sister Albert's office was high-ceilinged and poorly lit. For some insane reason, she was running the air conditioner, even though it was kind of cool. It was probably some technique to make us confess. Maybe a leftover from the Spanish Inquisition.

Sister Albert herself was an enormous, boxy woman with a square head, square fingers, square torso and square man-boobs. My deepest fear in dealing with her was that on one of these visits, she'd say, 'Okay, Miss Jarvis, enough talking. We're going to settle this with some good old-fashioned wrestling. Get on the floor!'

I don't really know why I thought that. I'm told I have an overactive imagination.

'Sit down, Miss Jarvis,' she said.

I sat down under the huge latch-hook rug portrait of the Virgin Mary that covered the wall across from Sister's desk. On the desk itself was a very fat manila folder, which I knew at once was my personal file. I could see layers of strata detailing my various types of offenses and achievements — many inches of pink paper, a few inches of green. Pink was disciplinary report paper; green was for academic achievement records. Just looking at my folder, I realized that it wasn't something you read — it was just something you *weighed*. Sister opened it and shuffled through the papers a bit.

'These are your records, Miss Jarvis.' She looked up and fixed me with a stony stare. 'You have a reputation for questioning and mocking this school and everything it stands for.'

'I don't mock,' I said. 'I just ask questions.'

'So, you are saying that you have nothing to do with this Poodle Club? Don't try to tell me you haven't heard of it.'

'I've heard of it,' I admitted. 'But I don't even know what it's supposed to be.'

'Jane,' she said, closing my file. 'Do you really want to be here?'

'Here, as in...'

'As in St. Teresa's,' she said. 'You have never really seemed happy here, never seemed like you fit in. We don't like to make anyone stay here who isn't committed to what our school stands for.'

'I'm committed, Sister. Totally committed.'

We listened to the air conditioner for a moment.

'We had to open your locker this morning because of the leaking,' she said. This was such an obvious lie that she had to turn away from the searching gaze from the latch-hook rug. 'We found this.'

She held up the crumpled flyer from the night before.

'We removed a display of these flyers last night,' she said. 'Would you care to explain why this one was in your locker?'

The truth was, I couldn't. But it was there, and I had to account for it somehow. And just saying I didn't know wasn't going to cut it.

'I found it on the floor this morning,' I said. 'I picked it up and read it. I'd seen them before, in the hallway one afternoon.'

It seemed wise to include that — to make it seem like I was laying all of my cards on the table. Sister definitely noticed, and one of her thick, square eyebrows cocked a bit.

'You've seen these before?'

'I was late a few days ago. They were in the hall when I went into class and gone when I stepped out.'

My honesty stalled her.

'All right, Miss Jarvis. You may return to your class. But I would advise you to watch your behavior.'

It seemed useless to point out that I hadn't done a thing.

Chapter 15

—⟨∽⟩—

A long with the standard three from Owen, there were three notes waiting for me when I checked my e-mail at the end of the day.

The first was official. Poodle Prom had officially been declared off-limits by the school — not that they knew where it was going to be, or when, or who was throwing it. Not that anyone was supposed to know about it. The message was written in a terse, no-nonsense voice that participation in 'the recently announced event' was forbidden. Which meant that Poodle Prom would definitely be the most popular, must-attend event in the history of the school.

The second was from Allison, asking me to meet her for coffee at a place called Pasquale's. The third had just been sent, and it contained the best news I'd heard in a long time. There was still extensive damage at both St. Teresa's and St. Sebastian's that required immediate repair, including a potentially dangerous electrical problem. Both schools would be closed the next day in order to bring in work crews.

Lanalee came bounding up to me.

'Listen,' she said. 'Had an idea.'

'What?'

'Let's just… join in. We'll start with something small. I thought about this all last period. How about, "Poodles wear them sideways"?'

'What does that mean?'

'I have *no idea*,' she said, stifling a laugh.

'Listen, Lanalee,' I said. 'If we get caught putting up flyers that look like those poodle flyers, we will be killed. I'm not kidding.'

'We won't get caught.'

'Lanalee,' I said, 'I know you want to help Ally, but we came really close last night.'

'Sister Charles saw three people with coats over their heads. Three inside-out coats, so she can't identify them.'

'Seriously. I can't explain how bad that would be for me right now. They already think I did it.'

'Okay,' she said, obviously disappointed in me.

I knew I was preserving myself, but saying these things made me feel like a traitor to all I believed in. Here was Lanalee, proposing a really good plan, and here I was, being all, 'Well, you know. School rules…'

But still. There comes a point where you know you have to play along, and I had reached it.

A half hour later, I was walking down Thayer Street to meet Ally when the suited man I'd met in front of my mom's restaurant stepped around the corner and practically right into me. He had a woman with him this time.

'Miss Jane,' he said. 'I had a feeling we might meet again during my stay. This is my companion, Claris.'

I don't speak Pretentious, but I figured that was just a way of saying 'girlfriend.'

Claris didn't seem like someone who would be with Mr. Fields. I think she was older — I could tell it from her eyes, her face — but she seemed younger. She was a little punkette, with black fishnets, short leather jacket, black leather skirt, high black boots. Her hair was a rainbow of frostings and tintings, so it was hard to say if it was brown or red or blond or copper or maroon. She was spiked as well, but her spikes were much longer than mine and shocked out all the way around her head in a series of thick points. She was small and clearly muscular — seriously athletic, in a dancery kind of way. But she didn't seem graceful, just hard. You sort of knew that if you touched one of those muscular arms, it would probably feel like a rat trapped in a bag.

'We've come to examine a bas-relief that's on special display at the university,' he said. 'A very fascinating piece from Byzantium. It strikes me that you might be interested in seeing it yourself. You seem quite a well-educated young woman. I speak as an experienced educator. I know a good student when I see one.'

This guy clearly had no intention of letting me go. He had a bad case of the chats-too-much.

'I guess,' I said.

'Incidentally, the lamb was quite excellent. Please tell your mother that we were extremely satisfied. We would certainly recommend The Pink Peppercorn. Wouldn't we, Claris?'

Claris looked deep into the Brown bookstore window, obviously not too interested in meeting a short high school student whose mom worked in a restaurant. 'It was good,' she said. But she didn't mean it. She said it the same way you say something like, 'The cable's gone out.'

Her eyes met mine in the window. They glowed white as they reflected off the lettering of a Brown sweatshirt. I turned back to Mr. Fields, who was beaming like an idiot.

'What brings you out today, Jane?' he asked. 'Just taking in this fine afternoon?'

'I'm getting coffee.'

'As are we. Perhaps we could get a cup together?'

'The dog has been in the car for a long time,' Claris said, wheeling around. 'We should get the dog.'

'Yes,' he said. I could tell he was annoyed, but he buried it. 'That is a good point. Our dog has been in the car perhaps a bit too long. He's not fond of the car. He sometimes enacts canine rituals on the seats as a form of retaliation. But there's time enough for a quick cup, I think.'

He smiled his small-toothed smile, and Claris openly rolled her eyes and turned the other way, this time looking into the slow-moving single lane of traffic in the road.

'Let's just get it to go,' she said. 'There's a Starbucks here.'

An almost-visible ripple of discomfort passed between them. I hate adults who have stupid fights in front of strangers.

'I've got to go anyway,' I said. 'I'm meeting a friend.'

'Ah!' he said. 'We won't keep you any longer, Jane. Maybe some other time, if fate throws us together. We are spending some time in this area, so this is quite possible.'

He bowed, and then he and Claris continued on their way. I hurried in the opposite direction, just in case he had a change of heart and just had to tell me something else.

'Wonderful,' I said to myself. 'Now I'm going to see this guy everywhere. I'm the luckiest girl I know. How much better can my life get?'

Chapter 16

Pasquale's was deeper into the Brown campus than we usually went. It took me a while to find it, since it was half hidden under a photocopy shop, with only a small blackboard and a clump of smokers outside identifying it. Edith Piaf was warbling in French over the stereo. There was an array of vegan cookies on display that looked disturbingly like dog biscuits. For entertainment, there was a shelf full of yellowing books and some Jurassic board games that you could tell were missing pieces without even looking in the box. A girl in a massive, checked head scarf was sobbing her eyes out at a table in the corner. Another girl walked in behind me carrying a tomato sauce jar half full of water. The jar had no lid.

This kind of thing isn't so unusual around Brown, which is filled with the Ivy League's most entertaining misfits. They like to hang out in places like this.

Allison was sitting primly to one side, two mismatched mugs in front of her. She was sipping from one very cautiously. She waved me over with a manicured hand, wrapped in an adorable pair of green-and-white-striped fingerless gloves. These went right up to her elbow, where they met the sleeve of a tight white angora sweater.

'I got you a drink already,' she said, pushing something steamy and vaguely minty in my direction. This movement sent our rickety table wobbling, and some hot brown liquid lurched out, dripping off the table and immediately onto my lap. 'It's a soy something. If there's anything else you want, I'll get it for you.'

She waved her hand at the counter, but then, realizing how unappealing the offerings were, withdrew it.

'I just wanted to go somewhere different to talk,' she explained. 'Somewhere private.'

She rubbed at the back of her left hand and smiled weakly.

'Okay,' I said. 'What's up?'

'All the things that I've been getting recently,' she said. 'They haven't been from my aunt. But you probably guessed that. You're smarter than me. I can't lie very well.'

'I thought it was strange,' I said. 'But why were you lying? Where's it from?'

She pressed her lips together, and they wobbled a bit.

'I got an... offer. That's all. I wanted to tell you, but I didn't think you would like it.'

'A credit card offer?' I asked.

'Not exactly,' she said. 'It's sort of a scholarship.'

'There are no scholarships for getting your hair colored, Al. There are no scholarships for sweaters.'

'No, listen,' she said. 'This is a special scholarship. They give me money for things I need — money for clothes, money to get my hair done, to go out. They believe in investing in image. They say it builds self-confidence and brings out your potential.'

'They? Who is they?'

'Just people,' she said, shifting the table nervously. 'Rich people who like to invest in the people they feel have potential but need some help.'

I leaned back in my chair just to the point where the back started to give, then came down with a thump, shaking the table again and sending soymilk foam everywhere.

'This sounds a little weird to me, Al,' I said. 'Where did you meet these people?'

'They came to school. And they liked me. And it's working, Jane. I feel good for once. I look good. I feel confident. Like the other day in class. Before, I would have just panicked when Sister Charles asked me something. But I didn't. I remembered what was in the book, and I gave the right answer. This is what I'm really like, Jane. I'm not stupid or ugly.'

'Of course you're not,' I said. 'You never were.'

'Yes, Jane. I was a freak. That's why I got left at the prom. Because I was ugly and weird. That's why I got nervous and puked all over that freshman. That's why every part of my life has been a failure.'

Her hands were shaking a bit now. She gripped the cup in front of her.

'That's why you're my only friend.'

I drew back at that.

'I don't mean *that*,' she said, grabbing my hand. 'You

103

know I love you. I just mean you're the only real friend I've ever had. No one else has ever seen anything in me. But these people do.'

'What's it called?' I said.

'They're called the Margarita Society. Not the drink. Margarita's an old name. They're not very public, just a bunch of private investors.'

Everything about this stank.

'I wanted to talk to you about something else,' she said. 'And you aren't going to like it, but just hear me out.'

'Okay...'

'I want us to do something like we used to do, you know, before?'

'Before?'

'You know, before. With Elton.'

This had taken a very unexpected turn. A lump suddenly developed in my throat. I felt like I'd swallowed a cork.

'I want us all to go to Boston, like we used to,' she said. 'All three of us.'

I took a long drink from my lukewarm, soy mint whatever.

'What for?' I finally brought myself to ask.

'Don't you think it's time we all tried to be friends again?' she asked. 'It's been six months, and I just thought...It would be nice, wouldn't it?'

Suddenly, all those things that Brother Frank had been saying to me, about things changing, about this year really mattering, they took on a heavy significance I could barely place. I sat there for a moment and chewed on my nails, my worse and oldest deep-thinking habit.

'I know this is hard, Jane,' she said, 'but please? It'll be great, I promise. We'll be like we used to be. It would mean a lot to me. After all, he was my friend too.

This was a low blow, but she was right. I couldn't stop them from being friends.

'You can go,' I said. 'I won't be mad.'

'It's not the same. It was better when it was all three of us. I promise it will be okay. We'll go tomorrow. We have the day off. You got the note, right?'

She examined her cell phone.

'I have to go in a minute,' she said. 'Just say yes? For me? Consider this the biggest favor you've ever done for me.'

My best friend's time was getting precious.

'Yes,' I finally said. 'Okay. For you.'

'Train station,' she said excitedly. 'Ten o'clock.'

'Where are you going?' I asked. 'Maybe we could do something tonight?'

'No, I have a... dinner. For the society. They make me go to a lot of dinners. But tomorrow!'

I sat there thinking for a moment after she had gone. If there were scholarship givers running around St. T.'s, I was fairly certain that Brother Frank would have known about them and would have told me. Unless that's what it was he was talking about... Maybe he was trying to warn me that there were rich strangers in our midst who wanted to pay for me to get a better hair color and to go to Harvard and get a pony.

No. People like this did not exist. Did they? Clearly, they did. And was that all Al had ever needed? A new sweater, some highlights?

There was that Fields guy. He said he was an educator, but he hadn't been anywhere near our school, and he never asked me about my studies. Nor did he hand me any large wads of cash. He asked about menus and historical things. He had asked me for coffee, but his partner had declined.

Had I been up for one of those scholarships and had I lost it? Had Claris just rejected me on the spot? That thought burned a bit. In all fairness to everyone, if the scholarship fairy was in town, then it should be flying though my window.

No. None of this added up. So there was only one thing to do — follow Ally to this dinner and find out what this was about. There was no need to feel weird or bad, I told myself as I bolted out of my seat and scanned the street. I had to make sure my best friend in the world wasn't getting herself into some kind of trouble.

Ally was just at the corner, getting ready to cross. I was half a block behind her. We walked down several bare-treed streets, past cars that were still dinged and porches propped up by wooden beams. We were just on the opposite side of the university, in an area I knew well but hadn't come to in months. House after familiar house.

We reached a corner that I hoped Ally didn't turn, but she did. This street was narrow, so it would be hard to hide myself. I didn't need to look to see where she was going, though. I already knew. She was going to the third house on the left. And when she knocked on the door, Elton answered it.

I felt my breath go shallow.

Okay. So she was meeting Elton. That made sense. She'd just asked me about him. And they were old friends. They were allowed. I thought about walking over to tell them both that there was no need to be so secretive. I had agreed to go to Boston already.

But my gut was telling me that there was a bit more to come. I had known from the moment she mentioned it. I thought about turning around to prevent myself from seeing what I suddenly knew I was about to see but couldn't. I had to watch it. I had to see it happen.

It was just a brief kiss as he was ushering her inside, but it said everything. It was comfortable, familiar. Definitely not the first time. It was the kind of kiss you have after there have been many more serious kisses, and now you can toss them around to say hello.

Nothing feels like betrayal. Nothing. It comes with an icy shock that stuns your whole spirit, physically rattles you. My knees started to give, so I leaned against a nearby car for support. I set the car alarm off. I didn't care. I knew it wouldn't draw their attention, even though I wished it had. For a moment, I thought I was going to be sick but forced the feeling down.

I needed to be somewhere else. Not standing here. I had to move. But I couldn't go home either. Anywhere else. A refuge where I could sit and think.

That's when I remembered the card. I almost tore my bag looking for it, but it was there, crushed down at the bottom with some paper crumbs and change — the little lilac card that told me where Lanalee Tremone lived. Just holding it, smelling the rose scent, reassured me. Lanalee was a girl of the world, and if anyone could help me, she could.

Chapter 17

Lanalee didn't live far — not in distance. She lived far in the sense of income range and taste. Her house was one of the grand old Victorians that dot the city. It was maroon and massive, with a circular glass-roofed sunroom attached to the side.

As I stood there on the porch, I felt the last reserve of the pure adrenaline that had pumped through me all the way here leave my body in one gasp — gone, like a ghost deciding the haunting was over. What was left was cold air and a horrible, hollow feeling the likes of which I'd never experienced. I gave the massive pineapple door knocker a few bangs, and a moment later, Lanalee was in front of me.

People always look different out of their uniforms. Lanalee looked a lot older, a lot more graceful. She was wearing a very tight and thin red T-shirt with a black lightning bolt on the shoulder and a slim black skirt. Her legs were bare except for a heavy pair of ringed tube socks, which slumped around her little green-bean-thin ankles at two different heights.

'Hey, Jane,' she said cheerfully. 'What's up?'

I said nothing. I just stood there shivering on the doorstep.

'Something's wrong,' she said. 'Come on in.'

She pulled me inside, slipping and staggering along in her stocking feet, leading me through to a massive living room — or rather a series of linked living rooms and dining rooms and sitting rooms that were connected by a few wide archways, making one massive room. The room had much too much furniture in it, and all of it was random, large, and from totally different historical periods. Our house was full of totally random pieces of furniture as well, but the effect was different. The Tremones said, 'We give money to museums from time to time.' Ours said, 'We baby-proofed once and never upgraded.'

'David!' she yelled. 'A girl is here! Be decent!'

'Who's David?' I asked weakly, looking around. There were several antique sofas, chests, vases, and table, but nothing that looked like it might be called David.

In reply, a pale hand holding a clove cigarette slowly rose from one of the low red sofas by the fire. Then a figure with jet-black hair that was as obviously dyed as my own propped himself up and gazed at me with luminous brown eyes and an utterly uninterested expression.

'My parents are away,' she said. 'It's just me and David right now. He's like a family friend. Don't worry about David.'

He smiled lazily and nodded at this.

'You look terrible,' she said. 'Sit down. David, go take a bath. We have to talk girl stuff.'

David stubbed out the cigarette and picked up an enormous glass of red wine. When he stood, he revealed himself to be as tall and lanky as his friend. Without a word, he walked past us and up the stairs.

'You don't have to—' I began.

Lanalee took me by the shoulders and pressed me into the warm sinkhole on the sofa that David had just vacated.

'He likes to take baths,' Lanalee cut me off. 'Believe me, you're doing me a favor.'

I had no idea what that meant or what kind of unlikely drama I'd just walked in on. There was a heavy, wrought-iron table between us that looked like it was made of pieces of old gates, sheeted with glass. Sitting on this was a platter of about two dozen cupcakes — a huge variety, all with pastel frosting and sprinkles.

'Did you have a party?' I asked.

'No, I just like cupcakes. Have a few. Want some wine?'

She held up a bottle.

'No thanks,' I said. But I couldn't fail to be impressed with the casual way in which she offered it. It looked like good wine, too — it had a yellowed label written in French, which was dated 1986.

'My parents have a cellar,' she said, noticing what I was looking at. 'They have cases and cases of the stuff. They don't mind if I have some. They think wine is pretty much a food. They're kind of European that way. You know — teach them to drink responsibly — that kind of thing. It's not a big deal.'

There was a creak on the stair, and David leaned down and looked at us.

'Lana…' he mumbled. 'Um. Do you have… um… soap?'

'Look in the cabinet,' she snapped.

He whipped his head back and disappeared.

'Okay,' she said, shrugging an apology. 'What's going on? Why so sad?'

She plucked up a cupcake and tore into it eagerly.

'I'm sorry I'm throwing this on you,' I said, feeling a little weird that I had crashed into this strange scene, with wine and wine cellars and bathing boyfriends. 'If you guys are having a…'

'Don't worry about David,' she said. 'Talk. Tell Lanalee. Lanalee fix.'

I opened my mouth but found myself uncertain as to where to begin.

'Allison…' was all I managed before breaking into a sudden and totally unexpected storm of tears. I mean, really — I had no idea where it came from. This prompted Lanalee to bound over and sink into the sofa next to me to wrap me in a lanky embrace. It took me a few minutes to get myself under control. I felt Lanalee playing with my spikes consolingly.

'I just saw Allison with my ex,' I said, sniffing hard.

'This is the ex you mentioned before?'

'There's only one,' I said. 'I mean, they can date. It's not like they're not *allowed*. But she knows how I would feel. That's why she was being so secret. She was sneaking off. Allison… sneaking.'

'Let's back up,' she said. 'Why don't you tell me about this guy? Purge. Only way.'

'His name is Elton,' I said. 'Andy Elton. We met freshman year. He's really... smart. He was the most genuine person. We were *friends*. We did everything together, the three of us.'

'So what happened?'

'I forgot that in the end, he was just a *guy*,' I said.

'They all are, dumpling,' Lanalee said sympathetically. 'Why did this one stand out?'

'I don't know,' I said. 'This is going to sound weird, but...'

I was about to tell Lanalee one of my deepest secrets. One that only Allison and Joan knew.

'I just never... liked guys. All of them seem so...'

'Juvenile? Dumb? Hygiene-challenged? Obsessed with one thing only? Stop me when you hear it.'

'Well,' I said, 'yeah. Kind of. But Elton was different. He was my friend first. We were friends for two years before we started to date.'

'How long did you go out?' she asked.

'Seven months. And two weeks.'

'And he broke up with you?'

'He said he thought we should really be friends,' I explained. 'Except that he hasn't spoken to me since that day.'

'Weak,' she said.

'There's more,' I said, torn between wiping my nose and ripping the paper off a cupcake. I went for the cupcake, and

Lanalee actually reached over with a napkin and dabbed at my nose for me, like my mom used to do when I was little. 'Allison's joined something weird. I don't exactly know what it is, but it's some kind of group that's giving her money.'

'What kind of *group*?' she said.

'She called them private investors. People who give out scholarships. But it's not just money for school — it's more for getting her hair done, money for clothes. She said they came to school and picked her out to help her develop her potential.'

'You win best story of the day,' she said, pulling at a handful of hair thoughtfully.

'And Allison wants me to go to Boston with her and Elton tomorrow. So what do I do?'

'Some cagey moves here,' Lanalee said thoughtfully. 'There has to be a reason for that — something big. Tell me this, do you hate her? Right now?'

'No,' I said.

'Be honest. You're entitled to what you feel.'

'I could never hate her,' I said, wiping my nose with a napkin. 'I just can't believe this. I have no idea what's happening in my life. It's like everyone made a pact to be weird.'

'Well, one thing seems clear. You have to get to the bottom of this. Go with them tomorrow. You need to find out more about what she's doing. You're the smart one, Jane. She needs you.'

'I guess,' I said, without much conviction.

'It's just one day. It's not like it will kill you. And you can call me if you're having problems, and I'll help you. I'll be like that person back at headquarters who talks you through things.'

As torturous as it was, it was a help to have Lanalee. She really did seem to have a broader, more balanced perspective — like she'd seen it all, done it all, and worn the T-shirt out. That was Bobbin for you.

'One day,' she said. 'Won't it be worth it if it gives you all the answers?'

Chapter 18

⁓⟳⁓

Ever hear those stories about people forced to dig their own graves at gunpoint?

On the entire train ride to Boston, I sat across from Elton and Ally and dug my imaginary grave. I considered the length of the shovel handle, how long it would take me to climb out of the hole, just how much satisfaction I would derive from showing dignity in the final moments of my life.

I always used to wonder about whether or not I'd do it. I think I'd probably throw down the shovel and say, 'You do it. You're going to shoot me anyway.' But then again, if you dig really slow, you get to live that much longer. And there's always the possibility that you'll figure out a really clever way of evading your captors, probably by whapping them with the shovel or throwing dirt in their eyes.

By the time we got into South Station, I had decided that I would probably start a refusal speech, but then they'd lower the barrel of the gun at me, and I'd immediately crack and start crying and begging. Then they'd shoot me before I was done, just to get me to shut up.

It's the worst ending to the scenario, but I knew it was the most accurate one. At least for the way I was feeling at the moment.

I was doing it. I was on the world's worst fact-finding mission. There they sat across from me, not knowing that I knew about them, pretending to be innocent. Elton looked formally uncomfortable, like someone had an antiaircraft weapon trained on his seat, which they would fire at any point if he made the wrong move. He also looked good, long and lanky with an untucked striped dress shirt. He always made an effort. Elton ironed if he felt it was necessary. He was that kind of a guy.

And Allison, whose idea this was, sat silent. She was blue pale, like the color of fat-free milk. An elegant blue pale, offset by a deep blue dress and black boots. I hadn't dressed for the occasion — I just had on a gray chunky knit sweater and jeans because it was cold. I felt grubby and small next to Allison.

'So,' Elton said, 'what do you guys want to do? Lunch?'

'Sure,' Allison said, not turning from the window. 'Whatever you want.'

She was completely absolving herself from responsibility for this situation. She kept her eyes fixed on the rolling view, as if she was trying to drink it all in — all the convenience stores, train station parking lots, the backs of housing developments. It was as if she hadn't asked me to come here, hadn't said that Elton was her friend too. She was barely with us.

Elton put on his headphones. The only thing I had in my bag was that stupid vampire novel, so I opened it on my lap and stared into its pages, occasionally flipping one for show. My eyes burned. My heart struggled to get out of my chest. I kept reflexively balling my sweaty hands up. But I managed to keep my composure.

It was a cold, stern Tuesday in Boston, and we arrived with no better idea of what we meant to do than what we started with. We ended up at Quincy Market, a former major Boston landmark with a four-column Greek façade, now a mall with a long, fancy food court. We split up in search of food. Allison only wanted a chai tea. Elton went for a heavy curry. I had no appetite but didn't want to be seen as the bitter ex-girlfriend who refused to eat. I ended up with a clam roll because the seafood place was the only one without a line. As soon as we sat down, Ally excused herself, leaving Elton and me to our lunches.

He dug into his curry. I rearranged my clam roll a few times and tried a few bites but soon gave up the effort. Elton set down his form. We looked at each other.

'So…" he said. 'This is awkward.'

'All part of the new Allison,' I said.

'I think she's just kind of growing into herself,' he said.

'I'm just saying. New clothes, new friends…'

'What new friends?' he asked.

So, Elton didn't know anything about this society. Well, obviously, I had to tell Elton about this. Elton was perceptive. Elton would have insight. And Elton and I would have something to talk about. And we would save Allison together from the clutches of weirdos. And then we would…

One step at a time, I reminded myself.

'She's met some people,' I said. 'I've been kind of worried about it. They're giving her money. They say it's a scholarship, but…'

'Oh, I know she got a scholarship.'

That deflated me a bit. But I pressed on.

'No,' I said. 'They're funding her in all kinds of weird ways. Giving her money to buy things like clothes, purses, a new cell phone. That's where all of her new stuff has been coming from.'

'They don't give out scholarships for that,' he said, looking over with a slightly cocked eyebrow.

'*That's* my point,' I said. 'Doesn't this make you kind of worried?'

'Her aunt gave her some money for clothes,' he said, spearing a curry-stained potato with his fork. 'And she got a scholarship.'

'It's not from her aunt,' I said again, much more firmly. 'Don't you see? She told me it wasn't her aunt.'

'She told me it was.'

'Then she lied to one of us,' I said, leaning back and pushing my tray just slightly in his direction, in an act of minor defiance.

Elton shook his head and chomped down a few quick bites of curry. Then he tapped the fork thoughtfully on the side of the black plastic plate.

'Don't you think you probably just misunderstood her?' he asked.

'That's a big misunderstanding,' I said. 'I'd have to be really stupid to get that confused.'

'People make mistakes. But okay — so what if you're right? What if she did get a scholarship like that? You should be happy for her. I don't see why you're not. Why are you just trying to pick everything apart about it? Is it because *you* didn't get it?'

This was more than I could bear. It was so wrong.

'You think I don't know,' I said, tears burning at my eyes. 'But I know. I *saw* you.'

He knew. All annoyance fell from his face and was replaced by a truly horrified expression.

'Jane,' he said. 'Look...'

I couldn't take it.

'Here,' I said, pushing the clam roll at him. 'Take it. Just take everything.'

I went directly to the bathroom. It was time to get this out in the open. Allison was there, gazing into the mirror, touching her face with the tips of her fingers, making small circles on her cheeks, admiring herself with a silent awe.

'Jane,' she said, not turning around. 'I'm glad you're here. We should talk...'

She leaned herself against the wall. She was getting a little thermometer-headed, pale right up to the hairline.

'I've made a terrible mistake,' she said, 'and I can't fix it. I thought it would all be okay if I was here with both of you because you two can fix anything. But I realized on the train that you can't fix this. You can't even talk to each other. This is pointless.'

Slow tears began to dribble down her face, ruining her perfect makeup. I took a heavy breath, and it staggered in my chest.

'I know,' I said. 'I know all about it.'

'You do?' she said. Her eyes grew bright.

'Yes. I saw you. I followed you.'

'Followed me where?'

'To Elton's.'

'Oh. Yeah. I should have figured that.'

Her chin sank, and she seemed instantly bored with that topic. I wasn't quite expecting that reaction. I was expecting more of a dropping to the knees and begging for forgiveness. Instead, she went to the window and pushed it open with the flat of her hand. A sharp burst of cold air came in, and she breathed it deeply.

'I need your help,' she said. 'I need you to talk to her for me.'

'Talk to *who*?' I said, wiping at my eyes with the back of my hand.

'Her.'

'Her who?'

'The demon,' she said matter-of-factly.

All of my personal trauma dissipated, and I stood very still. Things had just changed. They had gone in a very unexpected direction, one that I immediately knew we wouldn't be returning from for a long time.

All I could think to reply was, 'The demon is a her?'

Not, 'What the hell are you talking about?' or, 'What size rubber sack do you think they'll put you in?'

'She is right now.'

'And she's... nearby?' I asked.

'She's at our school.'

'Right,' I said.

'I traded my soul, Jane,' she said.

'Right.'

'I did. This is not a joke.'

'I'm not laughing.'

'I signed a contract,' she went on. 'I was desperate. But there's still time if you talk to her...'

I'd read somewhere that there is really no such thing as 'crazy', that we all slide along a scale of acceptable behavior and thought. But when someone starts telling you that they've been talking to demons — this is a sign that they've gone down the slippery slope to the far end of the scale. You are supposed to take them by the hand and escort them back to their seat in reality or find someone who can.

'I know you don't believe me,' she said. 'I was afraid of this.'

She pulled a small medicine bottle out of her purse.

'I took these from my mom's bathroom cabinet this morning,' she said. 'I don't want to... but I have to take them.'

'What are they?' I asked.

'Penicillin.'

This would have little impact on most people, but it meant a lot to me. Allison was allergic to penicillin. One pill could probably do her serious harm. More than one would kill her for sure.

This is one of those moments in life that I fell like certain 'very special episodes' of television shows and well-meaning school counselors try to prepare you for, but nothing can get you ready for an actual emergency. These moments aren't backed up by musical sound tracks and careful camera angles. This was just me, in a Boston bathroom, my best friend holding a bottle full of a substance that was incredibly toxic to her.

'Allison,' I said, 'give those to me. Put them in my hand.'

I held out my hand as far as I could without moving from my spot and spooking her.

'She doesn't believe me,' Allison said quietly to the void. 'If Jane won't listen, no one will listen.'

'Come on,' I said again. 'Give those to me.'

She popped the top off the bottle.

'Don't come any closer,' she said. 'Go.'

I had twelve thoughts at once. I would call 911. I would call my dad. I would call Lanalee. Strangely, it flashed through my mind to call Owen since he was clearly waiting to hear from me. I would bound across the room and snatch the bottle and take them myself. The ceiling would fall down, knocking them from her hand.

'Go,' she said. 'I don't want you to watch.'

'I'm not going.'

'Okay.' She dropped three of them into her palm. I could see she was shaking now. 'I'll take them if you *don't* go. I shouldn't have told you. I shouldn't have gotten you involved. Just *get out.*'

She held the pill an inch from her bottom lip and glared at me through watery eyes. I had no choice now. I bolted out the door and into the food court. I skidded back to our table, where Elton was scowling at my clam roll.

'Get up!' I said. 'It's an emergency!'

'What?'

'Allison's threatening to kill herself.'

'*Kill* herself?' he repeated. He looked around the food court, obviously thinking what I would have thought — people don't threaten to kill themselves in places like these. They get cheese fries instead and opt to do it more slowly, on a thirty-year plan.

'She's got a bottle of penicillin,' I said. 'That's why she brought us here. She's threatening to take them.'

He needed no further explanation. He was up in a shot.

We arrived in the bathroom to find that Allison was standing in front of the mirror, twisting up a lipstick.

'Al,' I said, immediately quieting down. 'It's okay. We're both here now. Tell me you didn't take them.'

'Take what?'

'Those penicillin.'

'I can't take penicillin,' she said. 'It would kill me.'

Elton threw me a baffled look.

Was my mind playing tricks on me? Her eye makeup was a bit smudged and her eyes were red, but otherwise, she was totally calm. Maybe this is what suicidal people were like — switching moods on a dime.

'I want you to give me the bottle,' I said. 'Come on now. You know we care about you.'

'What bottle?'

'You know what bottle.'

Elton was glancing between us, deciding which story seemed more plausible.

'There is no bottle,' she said. 'If you don't believe me, here.'

She held out the tiny Coach bag. Elton stepped forward and took it. He pulled out the cell phone, a small wallet, some keys, and an eyeliner. He turned it upside down and shook it and then carefully replaced everything.

'They could be anywhere,' I said. 'They could be in the trash.'

'There are no pills,' Allison said. 'Jane, why are you saying this?'

Elton had made up his mind.

'I'm going,' he said firmly. 'I'll meet you out there, Al.'

She nodded, still looking adorably confused by the whole thing.

'What are you *doing*?' I said.

'Jane,' she said, her face falling. 'Just forget everything I said, okay? And what I did.'

'What do you mean, *forget* it?'

'Don't get involved. I don't need you to. I don't want you to. I want you to go. Just go. I promise I won't hurt myself, but go.'

So I did.

Elton was waiting just outside the door, holding my bag.

'That was not okay,' he said, passing it to me. He wouldn't even look at me. 'If this was some kind of trick to get us back together or something, then it was sick and it didn't work. I think you should leave.'

Both of them were telling me to go, and both seemed to mean it. So I put my bag over my shoulder and left.

Chapter 19

Here is a simple psychological trick that I first developed when trying to get over my fear of getting blood drawn. It works when you are confronted by anything horrible.

First, when the horrible thing or idea comes near you, force your mind to go blank. Turn out all the lights. Try to tell yourself not to think about anything. Your brain hates total darkness and silence — it won't let this go on for more than a second or two before it starts rummaging around in the closet and throws the first thing it gets its hands on at you.

Try it now. You'll see.

When I first developed this, the thing it threw at me was the theme song to *Friends*, which I happen to hate for its relentless cheerfulness and organized hand-clapping. But that's what I got. And when you get this random offering from your brain, accept it. It is your mantra now.

So, something horrible happens, like when I have to get my blood drawn, I take my mind to the quiet, dark place and play the *Friends* theme at top volume. I give it all my concentration. I crank it up if I start becoming aware of the rubber tourniquet that they tie at the top of your arm or the nurse poking around my antecubital space. (This is the technical name for the underside of your elbow, where they usually get the blood from; knowledge is also a great defense against illogical fear.) I'm surprised they can't hear it. Sometimes, I think I even mouth the words, and one time, I know for certain I tapped out the claps with my free hand.

I don't remember getting on the T. I just kept walking until I must have come to a station, found a token, and gotten on. Before I knew it, I was stumbling out at the Harvard Square stop, into a mass of people and a hard and kicking fall wind.

I felt what seemed to be a twelve-inch split open up in the middle of my chest. I wrapped my arms around myself and pushed through the crowd, who were behaving as consistently as the blowing leaves — oblivious to everything because they were talking on their phones and their scarves were whipping up over their eyes. They were wandering into traffic at the wrong times, even though they give you about fifteen minutes to cross the street in Boston and have a countdown timer to guide you. There was just general confusion in the air, and I was cutting through it, forcing control into my every step. I had thick Frye boots on, and they crunched hard on the leaves and struck solidly on the brick.

'Think,' I told myself out loud. 'Think.'

The bracing wind cleared my mind a bit and took

away some of the nervous burning in my skin and stomach — a bit. Harvard was a good place to make yourself think. The heavy iron gates and the brickety-brickness of it all... it reassured me that world was solid and stable, and Ally was just ill, and there were cures for illness. I would just tell someone, and they would get her the right pills.

I turned sharply into one of the Harvard courtyards, where space is a bit more free and people usually run into you while jogging, or their dogs leap into you Superman style as they try to catch Frisbees. The square was almost empty. Behind me, I heard the faint tickity-tickity-tickity noise of a bike.

I stopped cold and turned on the heel of my boot.

There, in front of me at about twenty paces, was Owen. He was leading his bike and coming in my direction. He looked blown by the wind. His pale, high-boned cheeks were worn red. He rolled the bike closer and came up to me. I set my lips and looked up at him, and he seemed to understand that this time, it was not okay. This face-off continued in silence for a good minute while the one dog on the common made a beeline for us.

I was about to shout at him, to tell him to go away, but he spoke first.

'Is Allison talking about demons?' he said.

A few minutes later, we were sitting in one of Harvard's countless coffee shops. I don't remember which one. My freshman stalker and I had two hot chocolates in front of us. I watched a mountain of whipped cream melt and sink into a chocolate sea, then I turned my attention out the window, to the rush of Harvard students blowing past.

'How did you know?' I finally asked.

'I know lots of things,' he said. 'If you'd called, I could have told you.'

'Or you could have just told me.'

'If you had called.'

'Enough!' I held up my hand. 'What do you know?'

There was a black pointy hat perched on a pumpkin in the shop window. Owen pointed at it.

'That's where it starts, really,' he said.

'With a hat?'

'With witchcraft. Or with something that happened right around here, maybe four hundred years ago, involving witches…'

'The Salem witch trials?' I put my head in my hands. 'Don't mess with my brain today, Owen. Seriously.'

'Hear me out,' he said. 'It will all make sense. Do you know what happened at Salem?'

'Of course I do. If you grow up anywhere near Boston, you *will* be taken to Salem for a field trip. It's the law. You *will* go to the Salem Witch Museum. You *will* buy obligatory souvenirs from the local witch shops. You *will* come home either wearing a pointy hat or a pentacle. I have both. Get to your point.'

'I am. Just listen. So, what happened at Salem? Tell me.'

'A bunch of girls started freaking out,' I said. 'The residents thought there were witches in town, possessing them with devils. They started accusing people of witchcraft. There were trials. A whole bunch of innocent people died.'

'Right,' he said. 'And do you know why all of that happened?'

'There are a few theories,' I said. 'Some people think the whole thing was caused by some poisonous mold — something that makes people hallucinate. Most people think that the girls were bored, they were messing around, and they started something they couldn't stop. It was the power of suggestion. But that was in 1692. They believed in devils then. They had manuals on how to get ghosts out of your house.'

'Yeah, but the power of suggestion doesn't change,' he said. 'It's used all the time. Advertisers use it. We see commercials all the time and we think they do nothing — but then we find ourselves wanting the stuff in them. Stage magicians. Cults. Government agencies. They all use suggestion. The mind is powerful. People can lift cars when they have to. Monks in Tibet can perform almost superhuman feats through the power of concentration.'

I chewed on the fringe of my scarf.

'So what *exactly* are you telling me, Owen?' I asked. 'This is 1692 all over again and some insane Tibetan monks have infiltrated our ranks?'

'No,' he said. 'I'm saying that what happened at Salem isn't actually that hard to re-create. Go back. When did all of this stuff with Allison start?'

'It was around Big-Little, after Al threw up.'

'Why did she throw up?'

'I don't know,' I said. 'Heat. Eating too fast...'

'Eating what?'

'A cupcake.'

A tiny bulb in my head went *boink* and suddenly, there was illumination. It was faint, but it was there. A cupcake.

'Easiest thing in the world to make someone throw up,' he said. 'Ever hear of syrup of ipecac?'

'We used to keep it around our house. My sister used to eat the air fresheners sometimes. Instant vomiting. But why would someone do that? Who would do that?'

'Why…because you end up with someone who's truly sad and desperate. And then you play with them. Who… someone rich. Someone bored. Someone smart.'

It suddenly smacked me right on the forehead.

'Lanalee,' I heard myself saying. 'She came into the bathroom. Right after it happened. And she took Ally as her big. She seemed so nice.'

He fixed me with a steady stare.

'Did she do this before?' I asked. 'At Bobbin?'

'Yeah, she's done it before. That's the basic plan. She more or less ruins someone's life. And then she walks in and says, I can help.'

'Okay, but…' I stabbed the remaining whipped cream iceberg and sank it. 'She does this how? She says, I can help… I'm a demon? Allison was sick, but she didn't lose her mind.'

'I think she starts it as a game,' he said. 'But then people start to feed into it. She probably bought her something to make her feel good. The new image boosts Allison's self-esteem, and from there, she begins to believe…

She feeds on her own energy. The more people respond to her, the more confident she gets. The more things go right, the more she believes what Lanalee told her.'

'There's this Poodle Club thing that's been going on at our school,' I said. 'That has to be her too.'

'I heard about it. That's her. She must be trying to screw around with a lot of people. And she's got a lot of friends. Maybe they're doing it together...'

'She's got *my* friend,' I said firmly. 'She's got Ally wrapped up in some crazy role-playing game.'

'Just stay away from her,' he said. 'You can't get her in trouble. You'll never be able to prove she did anything. She's very smart. I've been trying to protect you.'

It was meant to be kind, sweet. Maybe even romantic. And I'm sure he meant it.

'Thanks,' I said, getting up. 'I appreciate the help. I'll take it from here.'

'Jane, *don't*.'

'Don't worry,' I said. 'I think I can handle Little Miss Bobbin. I'll write sometime, promise. You've just answered a lot of questions for me. I owe you.'

I got up over Owen's repeated objections. He even tried to follow me. His concern was touching, but I had to shake him loose. I lost him in the middle of Harvard Square by cutting through a tour group and headed back to South Station.

Chapter 20

The Town Car was in the driveway, and there was a warm, yellowish glow coming from inside the Tremone house. All of the windows were lit. The whole house was awake, alive. When I knocked at the door, it swung open in a moment.

Lanalee was dressed in long, sweeping black pants and a skintight black turtleneck. This outfit made her look extra tall. In my worn jeans and gray cable-knit sweater, I looked and felt all of two feet.

'I wondered,' she said. 'I figured that's what this Boston thing was all about.'

She left the door hanging open as an invitation to follow her into the house. We went back into the living room. She tossed another log into an already alarmingly large fire. The room was sweltering.

'So,' she said. 'How's Allison?'

'She threatened to commit suicide earlier today.'

'Huh.' Lanalee tapped her teeth with her fingernail and thought that one over for a moment. 'So soon...

Anyway. Wine? Soda? Sparkling water? And I think, for some reason, I might have a bottle of Yoo-hoo…'

She waved her hand toward a low table behind the sofa that had some bottles on it. A rage spun up inside me the likes of which I'd never experienced. My face set in a hateful stare.

'No drink?'

I continued to glower.

'Oh, please,' she said, throwing herself down on one of the sofas and grabbing a cupcake. 'Spare me. You look about as scary as a pissed-off parakeet. Do you know who I *am*, little girl?'

One thing you should never, ever do to me is call me *little girl*. But the glower had run out of steam, so I sat down very calmly.

'I know you've done this before.'

'I have.' She devoured an entire cupcake in one bite, swallowed easily, and smiled.

'You're behind the Poodle Club.'

'I *am* the poodle,' she said. 'That's true.'

'And you're messing withy my friend's head.'

'That's possible,' she said. 'But unintentional. I just came looking for a deal.'

'You told her that you were going to take her soul.'

'Is that all she told you?' Lanalee looked aghast. 'Ungrateful cow. It's not like I didn't give her anything for it.'

'And what did she give you?'

'I'll show you,' she said, leaning in excitedly.

She got up and went over to the mantelpiece, which

was covered in perfume bottles — all different colors and shapes. There was a long, narrow red one with gold threading cut through the glass. There was a tiny baby blue one, completely round. Another was blown green glass, another all yellow with a plastic daffodil top. She took a lavender-colored, heart-shaped bottle down from the back and center, where it had been prominently displayed. It was quite large. It had an opalescent finish, a green porcelain stopper, and a cameo of a woman in the center. It was a magnificent bottle.

'This is my last one,' she said, smiling at it. 'The rest are all full. I kept this one for the end.'

She turned the bottle in her hands lovingly.

'I'm told it's stifling. I'm told it's like being sucked into an underground pipe that's just big enough to hold you, your face pressed into the rusty metal, your lungs never able to expand to get a full breath of air, a trickle of water always running over you… total darkness… and no one knows you're there. You're just under their feet, maybe a foot or two under a city sidewalk, but you'll never be heard, never be found… and you'll never die. It will be like that forever.'

She signed contentedly.

'I have a journalist from the *New York Times*,' she said. 'I let him come out for a few minutes one afternoon and tell me all about it.'

She carefully replaced the bottle.

'There's nothing in the universe more desirable than a soul,' she said. 'People think bombs are powerful. Or money is valuable. Bombs cause little dents in the earth.

Money is paper. But souls… souls are impossible to create or destroy. Souls are living energy. Owning a soul — really owning it — that is the only real power in this world.'

'You must watch a lot of TV,' I said. 'I don't know what you guys are into, but she really believes this. It has to stop, and you have to back off.'

'It doesn't work that way,' Lanalee said, poking her finger into the pink frosting on her second cupcake. 'I can't just back off. We signed a contract. It's all legal. I need the soul. I can't just give her up.'

'I'm not playing along with your game, okay?' I said, losing all patience.

'It's no game, Jane.'

'Fine,' I said. 'In your little fantasy world, what will it *take* for you to give her up?'

'Now, *that's* an interesting question,' she said, putting down her plate and leaning forward. 'What are you offering me?'

'What do you want?'

'Well,' she said, 'the deal is still in the bonding stage. I haven't taken possession yet. I don't get her until the Poodle Prom on Halloween.'

'So you need to take possession of… someone? Is that it?'

'That's generally the way it works.'

'So take me.'

She looked at me, then at the heart-shaped bottle, as if sizing up whether or not I could fit in there.

'And what do you want in return?'

'Nothing. Just switch us.'

She examined her remaining cupcake for a moment.

'The thing that keeps this job challenging,' she said, 'is the fact that we can't just grab you and wring your soul out of you. If we kill anyone, we forfeit. No force, no threats. As little direct contact as possible. We can only try to coax you to do what you clearly want to do anyway. We can only take a willing soul.'

'I'm willing.'

'But you don't believe,' she said.

'In devils? In you? No, Lanalee.'

'That's no fun,' she said. 'But you do believe that something's happened to Allison. Something that's hard to explain. Something I did.'

'I think you made her think something was going on. There. Are you satisfied?'

'It'll do. Your opinion will change. Now, I always give *something*. That's what I'm good at! But in your case, we could do something better. How about a bet? I'll let Allison go right now. I'll set her free. The rest is just us. You win the bet — you walk away.'

'Fine,' I said. 'What's the bet? Where's your twenty-sided die? Let's get this going.'

'The kiss,' she said, 'is a very powerful gesture. So here's what I want. You get yourself to the Poodle Prom. I'll make sure Elton gets there. Once you're there, you have until midnight for him to kiss you. You can't tie him up and make out with him against his will. He has to give you a kiss.'

'And then?'

'And then you're free. You'll both be free. Can't get more fair than that.'

'And if I fail?'

'Then you go into the bottle.'

'Fine,' I said. 'Done.'

She almost clapped.

'I'll have to mark you,' she said. 'I have to make some sign of the agreement. I'll send you a more formal contract later on, but I need to leave something on the body.'

'Mark me how?' I asked.

'Just with a pen.'

Good. This was just what I needed. Something to show Allison that it was all over, that I had taken it on.

'Fine,' I said. 'Mark me.'

She grinned and picked up the remaining cupcake and more or less shoved it all in her mouth at once by taking these large, gulping bites, like a baby bird eating. Then she went across the room to a rolltop desk. She removed a key from a nearby pot, unlocked the desk, reached in, and produced what looked to be a very fine antique pen-and-ink set.

'If you could just take off your sweater,' she said, 'I'll do your arm.'

'No problem.' I yanked off my sweater. 'Have a preference?'

'Oh, the left one, please.'

I turned my left side toward her and pushed up the short sleeve of my T-shirt so that nothing would get in her way.

'That's perfect,' she said. 'Thanks.'

She dipped the pen carefully into the ink pot and let one or two drops leak out before coming near my skin.

'You're always supposed to use virgin parchment for contracts,' she said. 'I think this counts.'

'Just do your doodle.'

Lanalee's scary demonic mark was a small, very rough cartoon of a poodle, with curlicues for fur and a smiley face. She took the pen set back to the desk and carefully locked it up, then came and sat back down crossed-legged. She had a loose, happy expression — almost a kind of ecstasy. I folded my arms, leaned back, and met her gaze with my own.

'Congratulations,' she said. 'We're all set.'

'Call her and tell her,' I said. 'Tell her it's over.'

'There's no need.' She smiled. 'She'll figure it out on her own.'

Chapter 21

When I got home, I tried Allison's number a few times, but she didn't answer. Joan was out, my father left a message that he had to go into school for some kind of reception for a visiting mathematician, and my mother was at the restaurant. It was dark, and the wind was causing one long, low branch of our big oak tree to bump and scratch against the window.

I slumped in front of the TV but couldn't concentrate on anything. Of course, I wasn't worried about any pact I'd made, nor did I have any intention of showing up at Lanalee's stupid event and chasing my ex-boyfriend — now my best friend's boyfriend — around in circles all night. I had gone along with the whole thing as much as I felt I needed to, and now it was done. But I wasn't feeling well. I was achy and tired and my skin was warm. It had been a long day.

Crick was relentlessly pacing in front of the door, looking at me anxiously.

'Okay,' I said, pulling myself with great effort from the sofa. 'Walk. But then Jane is going to bed, okay?'

He hopped from foot to foot, like a tiny Irish step dancer.

Crick was too dignified for a leash. We called it a walk, but really we just opened the door and let him trot out. But when I opened the door, he didn't trot. He sat and stared in mortal terror at the fifteen or so cats that were on our porch. Then he hid behind my ankles.

The cats themselves were calm and still, some draped on the railing, others sitting primly. I recognized quite a few of them. Gray Betty from two doors down. Angelface from across the street. Hamlet, the kitten from the house that the Brown drama students were renting. The cats all looked up at me, their curious eyes glowing gold and green in the dark.

'What are you doing here?' I asked.

They didn't answer. Because they were cats.

This was deeply odd. I wasn't sure why the Cat Club had decided that our porch should be the rendezvous point for the night, but it did give me the uneasy feeling that something small, furry, and dead might be involved.

There was no way that Crick was going out there. Cats terrified him. A cat had jumped on his back once and ridden him like a camel, digging its claws in for support. I quietly shut he door, and Crick retreated to his special safety zone behind the television. This was fine by me. I was growing more exhausted with every second. I could barely drag myself upstairs, put on my pajamas, and get into bed.

My head began to spin the moment it hit the pillows. I had never been so relaxed in all my life. My bed had never felt so soft, my sheets so cool. I started to fall asleep so deeply, it actually felt like my head was falling through the pillow and into the mattress...

I barely jumped when I noticed the man on my bed. I opened my mouth to scream — but something in my head was saying, *Don't. It's no use.*

It was Mr. Fields, the man I kept bumping into. I looked at him, and he looked at me, an ecstatic smile on his face. He wore a black suit, a kind of Edwardian-looking cut, a bowler, and a pair of very round, green glasses. He had a long purple scarf wrapped several times around his neck.

'Jane!' he said. 'I'm so pleased! I had hoped all along it would be you. Here. Take this. This will help.'

He passed me a coat. I pulled it on and hugged it tight around me, as if it could protect me. Then he made sure I was securely propped up, with pillows behind and alongside me.

'Hang on,' he said. 'We're going for a ride.'

He pulled an object from inside his coat, which at first I thought was a flashlight made of a deep black plastic. He shook it hard, and a long silver tentacle of whip shot out of it. He snapped this at the foot of my bed.

I actually felt myself falling deeper into sleep, as if I was dropping through floors of a building, down, down, down — yet I seemed to be totally awake and lucid. And then we rose. Both of us and the bed too. The legs of the bed were extending themselves. Once they were about two feet from the ground, they began walking. The bed pinched itself up to get through my bedroom door and traipsed carefully down the stairs. Crick, who hadn't quite recovered from the cat incident, sat at the foot of the stairs and looked at me accusingly, as if asking me why I was doing this to his little doggie head.

'I don't think I'm well,' I finally managed to say.

'You're doing *very* well!' he said happily. 'One of the best reactions I've ever come across. But it doesn't surprise me one iota. Not one iota!'

'Thanks?'

'You're very welcome!'

'Okay,' I said. 'I know this isn't happening, so I'm not going to get upset.'

'Jane, dear, this is very much happening. But there is no need to get upset. You've made the very best decision of your life. And I'm here to show you what awaits you.'

Crick dodged out of our way as we reached the bottom of the stairs. He trailed us halfway to the door but then backed off. The cats scrambled out of the way as we crossed the porch. Now we were out on my street. I could feel the cold a bit, but it was distant. And though I saw the trees bending hard, I felt no wind. The bedposts grew very long, and with every step, they grew a bit longer. By two blocks down, we were as high as the housetops. As the bed clip-clopped its way down the hills, the legs grew longer still.

'Here,' he said, shoving the whip into my hands. 'Would you like to steer?'

'No.'

'That's all right. It knows the way.'

We went down, deeper into town, to the rivers that

separate East Providence from downtown. The bed stepped easily over the rivers — one, two — and then we were downtown, level with the tops of the very highest buildings.

'Sit tight for a moment,' he said. 'This next bit can be disorienting.'

There was a cracking sound, and I felt my head jolt forward with extreme force. The moon winked out for a fraction of a second and was replaced by a gold chandelier the size of a motorcycle dangling above us. My bed had returned to its normal height and sat in the center of a long room. The walls of this room were entirely mirrored with slightly rose-tinted glass, so we saw ourselves again and again. The floor was black-and-white check, and that too was reflected, making the room seem endless. I felt like I had seen this room before somewhere, possibly in a textbook or a documentary. It was palatial, with furniture decorated with embroidered scenes and gold leaf running along its edge. People rested on some of the furniture and turned to look at us with great interest.

'Sorry about that, my dear,' Mr. Fields said. 'Claris? Give me a hand, will you?'

Claris was standing by the foot of the bed. She was dressed in a severe black suit, cut so sleekly to her frame that you could almost see her elbow joints. The front of the jacket was extremely low cut, revealing a delicate black silk shirt bound together by a series of massive silver safety pins. She walked over and stiffly extended her hand.

'Stand up,' she said.

'Be polite,' he said to her sternly. 'Jane is an honored guest now.'

Claris looked reluctantly contrite.

'May I help you?' she said.

'I think I'm fine here,' I said.

She looked to Mr. Fields.

'Let her sit,' he said. 'Jane doesn't have to get up if she doesn't want to.'

'Who are these people?' I asked.

'These,' he said sweeping his arms around, 'these are *heroes*, Jane! These are your peers now. Let me make a few introductions. Over there...'

He pointed to a haughty-looking threesome, all dressed in scarlet velvet.

'The Borgia family of Rome. One of history's greatest political dynasties. Wonderful people. Next to them, with the rather large hat, that's King Ashurnasirpal II of Assyria. He set new standards on how to deal with your enemies. He covered an entire column with their skins. Some of the enemy soldiers he walled up while they were still alive — he put others into pillars, also while they were still alive. Very, very effective. Had one of the greatest libraries in all of history. We owe him a great debt. It's because of him that we know much about the ancient world.'

The man next to the Borgias mumbled something in what I guess was Assyrian.

'Maybe I'm having an allergic reaction to something,' I said.

'This is reality,' the man said. 'You've always known, haven't you, Jane? You've always known what you're capable of. It was never hard for you, any of it, was it?'

I said nothing. I just sat there on my bed, with my lunatic buddy with the green glasses. But I did feel something inside me — a sense of knowing. It always *had* been easy. School. Grades. If I wanted to understand something, I did.

'Exactly,' he said. 'You know. It was only a matter of alerting you to what was already inside you. We cannot go much further now, Jane. This is only a glimpse. The full view is coming. For now, goodbye.'

The cracking noise seemed to come from the inside of my head this time. Blackness for a moment. Then we were reversing our path past unlit windows and signs, jumping backward over the rivers. We got lower and lower as we hit my street, lower still as we re-scattered the cats. Then, when we reached the front door, I felt the ground give out. It was more than just a hole — it felt like matter itself was being erased from that very spot, taking my consciousness with it. I had just enough time to remember that they say that if you fall in a dream, you almost never experience the moment where you hit the ground unless you die. But how anyone would know that is hard to say because they'd have to be dead to have that information…

I smacked into something and the falling stopped.

I sat bolt upright.

I was sprawled on the living room floor with an old issue of *American Scientist* wound tight in my grip, and I was wearing one of my mother's old winter coats. It was morning. Joan stood over me, eating a muffin and poking me with her slippered foot.

'Are you drunk?' she asked.

I released the magazine and reached up and felt my face. I seemed to be alive and sober.

'I don't think so,' I said.

'Why are you sleeping on the living room floor, then? In Mom's coat? That seems kind of drunk.'

'I'm not drunk,' I said, groggily pulling myself upright. 'I'm just… thinking.'

'Oh.' My sister accepted that my thought processes were different from hers. 'You better get dressed. Oh, and I used all the hot water. Something's wrong with it. Sorry.'

She stepped over me and left. Crick came over and stuck his little Scottie snout in my face, licked my cheek, and then trotted off. With great effort, I managed to get to my feet and up the stairs into a shockingly cold shower. I rubbed my temples briskly, trying to wipe the dream away. My clothes had been slightly damp, and now I was cool. I'd most likely burned through a high fever during and night and now felt refreshed, alive.

As I scrubbed, I carefully preserved the poodle on my arm.

'At least that,' I told myself, 'takes care of that.'

Chapter 22

It was one of those crisp and perfect New England mornings, one of the few times that it's actually nice to live here. All the leaves had turned a bright gold, which stood in dark contrast to the sky, which was almost electrically blue. It provided a brilliant frame for the brightly colored Victorian houses that lined my street. Tons of rotting leaves covered up rotting, lost newspapers. People ambled along with their dogs. It seemed much sunnier than it should have been at seven thirty in the morning, and the chill in the air didn't even bother me as much as it normally would.

In short, everything was normal. Better than normal. No walking beds or Assyrian kings in sight. I had a quick shower and a bowl full of cold tuna steak with grilled limes and headed to school.

I decided to walk along Benefit Street, which is one of Providence's jewel box streets — an incredibly tight row of old houses, each one so painfully important and historical that it's plaqued and tagged up to the roof.

Benefit sits at the midpoint of an incredibly steep hill, walling off the drop. So, the owners of these million-dollar monuments get amazing panoramic views of the city and the river below them.

Walking down Benefit and looking over the city gave me a strange sense of… well, power. I can't explain it any better than that. I felt juiced up, alive, like I owned the whole city, everything in sight. It was all an echo of my dream, which still felt so real.

I remembered what Mr. Fields had told me that day, about the houses being bought with slave money, that there was a darkness underneath everything… and for a moment that clouded my thoughts. But then I didn't feel it anymore. It was just too nice a morning.

I realized that at this time next year, I'd be walking down a street in Boston, maybe on my way to class at Harvard, and that I wouldn't be wearing a brown polyester skirt, a worn and yellow white oxford-cloth shirt, or saddle shoes. I would be dressed like a human. The future was close. I could taste it. I even opened my mouth a bit so I could get an extra gulp of that fresh morning.

Allison was early too. She was lurking around the front gate. She seemed to be waiting for me, just like the good old days. She also seemed remarkably round-shouldered.

'Did you get my messages?' I asked.

'No. I can't work my phone.'

'Come on,' I said. 'We're early. Time for a coffee. On me.'

We walked down to the little coffee place a few blocks away, and I bought us some cappuccinos and heated chocolate chip cookies. Allison lumped herself down at one of the tables. I noticed, as the sunlight streamed in through the window, that her face was losing some of the glow from the facial. It looked a bit sallow. She barely stirred when I presented her with her breakfast. Lanalee's game was clearly taking its toll on her.

'Look,' I said.

I rolled up my sleeve and showed her the poodle. Her eyes lit up in instant recognition.

'Jane,' she said, 'what did you do?'

'I took over for you,' I said. 'I swapped places.'

'Oh my God,' she said. 'Jane, that's really serious. You made a bet? What is it?'

'It's not important.'

'Yes, it is. What is it?'

'It doesn't matter,' I said dismissively.

'What is it?' It was upsetting to see how seriously she took this stuff.

'She bet me to kiss Elton at the Poodle Prom,' I said offhandedly. 'Or, actually, that I have to get him to kiss me. Because we're twelve, right?'

She stared into her coffee.

'This is my fault,' she said. 'All of this.'

'Ally…' I took her hand from across the table. 'I know it seemed real, but it's not. And I'm going to prove it. You're safe. There's nothing Lanalee can do to you.'

She shook her head, revealing some very unflattering brownish roots under the glowing red sheen.

'I need to get out of here,' she said, pushing away her breakfast. 'I need air.'

Before I could stop her, she had staggered away from the table. I followed right after her. She was walking fast, then suddenly turned into someone's driveway. She went thermometer-headed. She held out her arms, holding me off. She staggered, holding her stomach. At the very last moment, she spun away from me. And then, out it came.

Paper. Ball after ball of paper. It was like that trick some clowns can do, where they appear to have many small balls or eggs that keep popping out of their mouths. Except this was a lot less amusing. This involved a lot of gagging and stumbling around. When she was through, Allison slumped to the ground and spread her hands over the pile, like a model on a game show presenting the new washer and dryer that could be mine if I won this round.

I stared at the many crumpled pages on the ground. There had to be at least twenty. I don't normally like to collect other people's vomit, but this seemed like a good time to make an exception to that rule. I picked up one of the closest pieces. It was cool, just ever so slightly damp — but not *nearly* as damp as it should have been. I uncrumpled it to find myself looking at something that seemed very familiar, some poetry. It took me a minute to realize that it was part of my least favourite thing in all of English literature — Tennyson's 'In Memoriam' — a three-million-page-long ode to a dead friend.

'You threw up a poem,' I said.

I collected a few more of the papers. It was more of the same poem — but what struck me was the fact that the text itself looked familiar. And then I saw on one of the pages, a small drawing of a fanged sheep — a little cartoon I used to make a lot in freshman year, especially in my English textbook.

I passed this over to her silently. She examined it.

'It's your English book,' she said quietly.

'No, it isn't. I destroyed that book, I hated it so much. I threw it in the Providence River on the way home after the last day of school. You were there.'

I looked at the pages again. It looked like one of my sheep. But still. That book was tossed into the river, where it sank. It slept with the fishes.

'That's not my book,' I said again. 'What is this? What kind of game are you playing?'

'I'm not playing a game,' she said weakly.

'Yes, you are,' I said. 'Ally, stop it.'

But inside, deep inside, there was a tiny, uncurling sprout of something terrible. Looking at Ally, looking at the paper on the ground, I suddenly felt my stomach drop out from under me.

Lanalee had a hold on Allison that I couldn't penetrate. She had somehow taught her how to do very strange things. And from the dream I'd had, it was clear that she'd gotten to me as well. There was only one course of action I could take now, one that went against my every instinct — I had to go to the authorities. I had to tell someone at the school what was happening. Brother Frank, I decided. He would believe the story. He would get a psychologist involved. He would fix this. I should have gone to him from the beginning.

'Don't go to school today,' I said. 'Go home and don't answer the phone until I call, okay? I don't want you going anywhere near Lanalee until I get some help.'

'You can't stop it, Jane,' she said. 'You shouldn't have gotten involved.'

'Of course I can stop it, Al,' I said. 'Leave it to me.'

Chapter 23

There was an unpleasant surprise waiting for me at school. Small red sparkly envelopes had been taped to many lockers. I walked past locker after locker and watched various people reacting to these mysterious notes. From their ecstatic reactions, I knew immediately what they were. The Poodle Club had made its choices.

Lanalee was waiting by my locker.

'Well?' she said. 'Satisfied?'

'Just stay away from her,' I said. I went to push her away from my locker, but she stepped aside easily and smiled.

'Oh, don't worry,' Lanalee said. 'I will. It's you I'm interested in.'

'Very spooky. I'm scared.'

'You know,' she said, 'I think you are.'

'I'm think I'm going to end this now,' I said. 'Your driveway won't save you.'

'Oh! Jane's going to tell on me! Now you've got me shaking. I wonder what they'll do to me? Gosh, Jane!'

She cocked her head dramatically and made a sad face.

'I guess we'll find out,' I said. 'They'll probably just send your sad ass back to the home for rich freaks.'

'No,' she said. 'I like it here. I don't think you'll tell on me. You like me too much. You really want us to be friends. And it would be such a shame if any unfortunate little fires broke out, wouldn't it? Fires can do so much damage, Jane.'

'Fires?' I said. 'You really are insane.'

'Oh no,' she said. 'Not insane. Ask your friend Owen about fires. He knows firsthand.'

But this was enough to make me stop. I needed to work this one through, to figure out exactly how serious Lanalee's threats were. She knew she had me, and she left it at that. I banged my locker shut and tried to walk away dramatically but instead walked right into Sister Rose Marie, who gave me a demerit for inappropriate care of school property.

'You know, Sister,' I said. 'I don't think I'm feeling so good.'

I must have looked pretty bad because she agreed.

As I schlepped my way home, feet dragging, it became clear to me that I was truly ill. Undoubtedly, I had caught one of the hundreds of bugs that go around Providence every fall.

The day didn't seem so nice anymore. The streets of Providence are steep, like I said, and the wind runs sharp along them. My skin was raw almost immediately.

Everything reeked of dead leaves. I went right to my room as soon as I got home and dumped my textbooks onto my desk. My American history book fell open.

All of it — every page — had thick black lines where the words were supposed to be. The pictures were gone completely and were replaced with squares that were so dark that they were almost impossible to make out, but looked like they had images of leering, squirrelly things with big tongues. Their eyes seemed to be following me.

I ignored that and kept flipping through quickly. Then I finally hit chapter 24, the one I was supposed to be doing for homework. There, where the picture of the Hoover Dam and the three related comprehension questions were supposed to be, were the following words:

You, Jane Jarvis, have entered into an official contract with a representative of the Satanic High Command, Hearth of the Cold and All-Consuming Fire, Destroyer of Worlds, Consumer of Souls, Taker of the Life Breath, Guardian of the Bottomless Ocean of Sorrow, Bearer of the Lance of Endless Pain, Lanalee Tremone, 10B

The thing that really caught my attention was the fact that they were written in fire.

As soon as I read them, the fire flashed up, and the whole book was consumed. And in the next moment, it coughed itself out in a tiny wisp of smoke, and then there was nothing left but a few flecks of history in the air.

Chapter 24

In the next second, my door flew open, and Joan was standing there.

'Are you burning candles?' she asked.

'No.' I stepped in front of the charred remains of my book.

'I smell candles. Do you have a lighter? Can I borrow it?'

'Go away, Joan.'

She noticed the smoke and remains behind me, and her eyebrows shot up.

'You burned your book?' she asked.

I opened my mouth to say no, I hadn't, it had exploded in flames all by itself and then put itself out. But even Joan knows that things don't happen quite that way. In an hour or so, she would have figured out something was wrong with that story.

'Yeah,' I said. 'I burned it.'

'Why?'

158

'I thought the way they represented modern political history was crap.'

'So you *torched* it?'

I have never seen my sister look so impressed.

'Would you burn my English book?' she asked.

'No. Why are you home?'

'I don't have a first period. I'm going in a minute. Why are you home?'

'I'm sick,' I said.

'With what?'

'Sickness.'

'Should I call Mom?'

'No,' I said, climbing under my blankets, coat, shoes, and all. 'I just need a little sleep.'

I huddled in my bed and tried to realign my world. I could make sense of this. I could. I *would*. One thing at a time. That's how you break a problem apart.

One, I had just seen fiery words leap from my book. Lanalee had promised me a fire.

'Okay,' I said aloud, 'there are things that cause flames like that. Chemicals… ones that react to air and start to burn.'

Difficult, but far from impossible. Owen said Lanalee had lots of friends. Maybe she knew people from somewhere like MIT — people who thrive on figuring out how to pull off little science tricks like that. Clearly, Lanalee was not only smart, but also a little unhinged. I was dealing with someone who took the risk of setting me or my whole house on fire. Who knew what else she was capable of to stage her little demon show?

159

Two, the dream I had about Mr. Fields... I'd had that right after visiting Lanalee. Most likely the result of fever. However, I couldn't rule out the possibility that Lanalee had slipped me something the night before. But how? I hadn't eaten anything there. I hadn't been jabbed with a needle. What contact had there been?

I looked at the mark on my arm. Of course. Drugs can be absorbed through the skin. The thing that was causing me all these problems was on my arm. I was riding the crests and dips of a drug reaction. Whatever drug I'd gotten was probably in my bloodstream by now, but it couldn't hurt to try to get it off me.

I spent the next half hour in the shower, scrubbing mercilessly at my arm, to no avail. The mark barely smudged. I stood wrapped in a towel in front of the steamy mirror and tried to rub it off with alcohol, peroxide, nail polish remover. Nothing.

I went back to my room and got back into bed in my wet towel. Owen had warned me, and I had ignored him. The only good thing to come out of this, besides the fact that I had got Ally out of Lanalee's clutches, was a good reason for not completing those three questions on the Hoover Dam.

The phone rang. It was Owen.

'Where are you?' he asked.

'Home,' I said, touching the ash. 'I'm not feeling good.'

'I was worried. I thought you might have—' He cut himself off. 'Listen, I have to show you something. It's really important. Meet me at the front gate of school

160

tonight, eight o'clock, right after it gets dark. I'll explain everything. Wear dark clothes. Come alone.'

He hung up.

At least my stalker still loved me.

Chapter 25

Here is a question you might be asking. 'Why, Jane? Why, after the day you had, did you meet your stalker under cover of darkness at the gates of your school, dressed in dark clothes and carrying a flashlight? Have you always had these Scooby impulses?

Well, yes. Yes, I have. I don't deny it. And after the day I'd had, anyone who wanted to offer up any explanations was more than welcome. So really, I don't know why you're surprised, if you are.

I stayed in bed for the rest of the afternoon. I have very little memory of it. My head was pounding, and my mom was in and out of my room checking on me. I woke up and looked around in confusion. I was still in my towel, my head right on the edge of the mattress.

I sat up sharply and looked immediately at my desk, hoping to see my book sitting there. It wasn't. Instead, there were charred remains. I slipped out of bed and brushed some of the ash aside. The flames hadn't touched my desk. It was completely unscathed. I got my trash can and scraped the desk clear until every last speck of soot was gone. I went downstairs and got furniture spray and came back and rubbed the spot raw.

My mother was at work, but my father was downstairs, grading papers. There was no way that he'd let me out of the house in the condition I was in, glassy-eyed and feverish, dressed all in black. I went downstairs in my pajamas and made a big show of telling him that I was just coming down for some water before going to sleep for the night.

Joan and I had long ago mastered the system of jimmying the locks on our bedroom doors, mostly by breaking them apart over the course of several years. I locked my door in anticipation of my parents coming to check on me during the night. I would just crack it open when I got home. The rest was just a matter of slipping out the back door, which proved to be no problem at all. In a moment, I was out.

As I walked to school, the sky seemed to be made of black marble. Just a hard surface. Cold. About to drop down on my head and crush me or box me in, like a sarcophagus. And at the same time, the chill sobered me up a bit and took away some of the dullness and pain.

We met and said nothing. With a nod, Owen jumped the gate, and I followed. We walked up the path slowly with our flashlights. The path, which is so nice and woody in the daytime, is the blackest, most twisty and scary stretch in the world as soon as the sun goes down. You can see *nothing*, but you can hear things rustling around you.

Sebastian's looked huge in the moonlight. Its golden bricks and white stone steps glowed, and there were still lights in some of the long, multi-paned windows. I felt very small standing in front of it. We weren't supposed to go over there except on supervised, official business, but it wasn't like I was committing a crime.

Well, I felt that way until Owen led me around through some of the bushes on the side, to a low window that was propped open. He went in first, and I followed and found myself standing on top of a display cabinet full of plastic models of the human ear and heart. It was some kind of lab, and even in the dark, I could see it was a lot nicer than anything we had. They had proper lab stations, not cast-off tables with random equipment on the side.

We moved into a hallway, which was heavily paneled in dark wood, past classrooms with doors paneled in smoked antique glass.

'This place smells like a sandwich,' I whispered. It was true. It smelled like a big, cheap meat sandwich. Generic bologna or something. That, with a little bit of shoe.

'And a little bit of shoe,' I added.

'I know.'

It just made me more annoyed. Give a nice building to guys and what do they do? They stink it up. It is an absolute truth that guys smell. Even Elton smelled a little.

We stopped at one of the smoked-glass doors, one chiseled with the words NO ADMITTANCE. Owen produced a plastic pouch, which he unrolled to reveal a set of very tiny screwdrivers. He ran a finger along these in what seemed like a very deliberate fashion, like he was showing off his spy skills. I have to admit I was impressed with what he did next. He carefully inserted the screwdriver into the keyhole, then leaned in and listened, making minute turns. A moment later, the door sprang open.

If I thought the path was dark, it was nothing compared to the ink-dark nothingness through that doorway. A pyramid comparison seemed apt. I had always wondered what it was like when explorers found the doorway into something that had been sealed and sunless for three thousand years.

Probably a lot like this. There was more dust and mold than breathable air and not one single photon of natural light. Once the door was closed behind us, Owen went into his bag and produced a much high-powered light, which helped a little.

We were in a basement, with a bunch of sagging boxes filled with old vestments, ancient issues of *National Geographic*, two broken bicycles.

'Wow,' I said. 'This is great.'

'Just wait a minute.'

He led me right up to the wall and then passed me the light. He started pressing on the wall, testing it, then had me focus the beam on a tiny spot.

'There's a door here,' he said.

There was a small hole there, which he worked at with his small screwdriver. A minute later, we were entering another room. I couldn't see much at first, but I could feel from the chill in the air and the echoing of our steps that we were in a large room. Owen went into his bag again and this time produced a few candles, which he lit and set down along the floor.

The room had a low ceiling and silvery walls. The floor was a mosaic of white, black, and red tile, and the ceiling was one huge painting of... impish things. Fire. Blood. In the center of the room was an enormous bathtub — similar to our own claw-foot tub but twice the size. It sat up on a slightly raised bit of the floor.

'What is this?' I asked.

'The guy who built this place, his name was Lazarus Fields,' Owen explained. 'He was a Satan worshiper, a student of Lanalee's. When she was alive, Lanalee was a grand high priestess of the largest Satanic order in the United States.'

'Fields?' I repeated. 'That was the name of the guy in my dream...He was a creepy guy I met in front of my mom's restaurant. He drove a little silver car...'

He went over to the tub and gave it a good, solid bang.

'See this? Ritual bathing. Satanists like to get naked and do things with messy stuff like blood and entrails.'

Owen leaned over and tested the knobs on the tub. Rusty, dank water coughed out.

'Still works,' he said, cringing at the color of the water and the numerous bugs that flowed from the tap. 'This is old-school demonism. Like having Allison cut her hair. That's an ancient way that someone makes a pact with a demon. The person offering themselves up gives the demon their hair. That's why they used to shave witches bald.'

'They did?'

'Yup. And then the demon turns the hair into hail. That's a sign of the pact.'

'Okay,' I said. 'You've showed me that a weird guy built the school, and I just met a guy who used the same name. There's no law against weird people building things. That's your proof that this is all true?'

'No,' he said, reaching into his bag and pulling out a gun, some kind of old six-shooter that looked like a prop from a Western. 'This is.'

And with that, he stuck the gun in his mouth and pulled the trigger.

Chapter 26

I had never seen death before. Funny how I could know it immediately, unmistakably.

Owen had been propelled backward and landed in the tub. The top half of his body sank, and his legs hung limp. On the wall behind, there was a long splatter line of blood. The dim light made it look like ink. There was a strange, hot smell in the air that somehow made me think of the inside of my teeth.

The whole thing took about five seconds.

I became very calm. I sat down on the foul, dusty floor because there was little else I could do. I stared at Owen's legs and the tiny river of water that seeped out of the tub and cut a brave path through the grime on the floor. The deafening echo of the shot was still painfully ringing in my ears, but I didn't put my hands over them to muffle the pain. I wanted my head to ring. It would have been worse if it was completely silent.

When the ringing subsided, I began to chatter to myself.

'Okay,' I said, hearing the wobble in my own voice. I steadied it. '*Okay*. Owen has decided to commit suicide in front of you. This is the kind of thing that leaves a mark on your psyche, so you're going to take this one step at a time, Jane. This is the shock phase. What you're going to do is sit and take a few good, deep breaths, and then you are going to go upstairs and get help. Okay, Jane?'

I felt myself nodding. I was amazed at the coherence of my own plan and felt reassured by it. I took a short, wheezy breath, then lapsed almost immediately into wild, choking gasps.

'Okay,' I managed to say when I stopped hyperventilating. 'Forget deep breathing. Just sit. It's okay. Just sit.'

I think I must have been sitting there for a good ten minutes or so. It was enough time for the blood on the walls to start to run a bit. When I'd had a chance to rest for a moment, I managed to get up.

The gun had dropped from Owen's hand as he fell. I gingerly picked it up and was shocked by its weight.

There was a tremendous amount of blood in the water, but I felt I had to try and see if there was anything that might be done. I carefully held the gun away from the edge of the tub as if I was afraid that he might somehow reach for it and do it again. I leaned over as far as I could. There was no question that Owen's head was completely under — so if he hadn't been killed by the shooting, he had certainly drowned by now. His one arm hung free. I felt for a pulse. There was clearly nothing. The arm was clammy, rubbery. There was no circulation.

Nothing. I let it go gently so that his knuckles wouldn't bang against the side of the tub. Stupid, but that's what I did.

'Why don't you set that down?' said a voice.

I turned to find Brother Frank in the doorway, his hands partially raised, as if he was showing surrender.

'There's been an incident,' I said. I don't know why I said that. *Incident?* What?

'Why don't you set the gun on the ground?' he asked. 'And we can talk.'

He said this cheerfully, as if he'd just come down to the basement looking for someone to have a chat with and was thrilled to find me there.

'There's been an incident,' I said again.

This was not what I wanted to say at all. I wanted to scream: OWEN HAS SHOT HIMSELF AND I SAW HIM DO IT. But my limbs were numb and it seemed like the only sentence I'd be able to say for the rest of my life was, 'There's been an incident.'

'Yes,' he said, still pleasantly. 'But why don't you put the gun down?'

I felt myself starting to say, 'There's...' I clamped my lips shut. Along with not being able to speak, I also appeared to be unable to move. I was half crouched, gun dangling from my hand, looking like I was either about to sprint or maybe leap into the air and perform a frolicsome dance.

'Jane...'

He stepped closer. I crouched a little lower.

Owen's foot twitched. Then the ankle flexed.

I found some new words.

'Jane,' I said quickly as my field of vision went black and white and spotty. 'Pass out now.'

And I did.

Chapter 27

When I came to, I was stretched out on the floor. There was something lumpy under my head, propping it up a little. I was looking at a ceiling. A very dirty old ceiling, painted in a hideous fresco of demons eating off one another's legs and pushing one another into lakes of fire. It was like a photo from a demonic travel brochure.

I twiddled all my fingers. I was not holding a gun. That was probably for the best.

Owen was standing above me, dressed in a terrible oversized sweatshirt with a shark wearing sunglasses printed on it. Brother Frank had his sleeve rolled up and was draining the tub.

'You okay?' Owen asked.

'I'm conscious, if that's what you mean,' I said.

'That's good enough for now.'

'Can you explain what I just saw?' I asked.

'That was me dying,' he said. 'A little.'

'What's dying a little?' I asked. 'That isn't something I'm really familiar with.'

'Well, I guess I'm what you would consider dead because I died once.'

'You're dead?' I asked, just to be clear.

'Yeah,' he said. 'Sort of. Not all the time. It's complicated.'

'Jane,' Brother Frank said slowly, 'you may have trouble accepting some of the things we are about to tell you.'

'Will I?' I said, my voice breaking into a laugh.

They looked at each other. I don't like it when people exchange looks in front of me.

'Get up,' Owen said, nudging me a little.

'No,' I said, stiffening. I put my hands over my eyes and tried my mind-blanking, *Friends*-humming trick. It didn't work.

'Get up, Jane. You can't panic now.'

I disagreed. This was the best excuse for panic I'd ever come across. I continued to panic and started making a kind of loud humming noise. Why, I have no idea. I just needed to do something. To hear something.

'Stop humming and listen,' he said, standing over me. 'I'm here to help you.'

'You said it was a game,' I answered. 'You said Lanalee was playing a trick. This isn't feeling like a game, Owen. I've played games. They are fun. This is not.'

'I know,' he said. 'I lied to you. I was trying to protect you. I didn't think you'd believe the real story, so I made something up to try to get you to stay away from Lanalee. That is the truth now, Jane. No more stories.'

'I'm not moving,' I whimpered. 'Leave me here. Rats will eat me. I'd like that.'

'Get up!' he yelled. 'Get up or I'll splash some of that water on you. You don't want that. Believe me. It's like centipede soup.'

I got up. I don't like centipedes. They are about 250 places above french fries dipped in ketchup on the spook-Jane-out scale.

'Perhaps,' Brother Frank said, 'we should continue this at the house.'

'I live with Brother Frank and the other brothers,' Owen explained. 'We'll have some privacy there.'

It was a quiet ride over to Brother Frank's house. He had an old tan sedan and had NPR on at low volume. A very boring man was talking about the merits of a book called *The Tiny Puddle We Call the Sea*, punctuated by dry little bursts of jazz music.

We arrived at a small, prim place that he shared with two older brothers. They were both sitting in front of the television watching the Discovery Channel and grading papers when we all trundled in. They seemed like they belonged to another world, and I was very jealous of them and their sanity. Nothing in the world seemed quite as appealing as checking tests and watching shows about grasshoppers — nothing.

But we didn't stay with them. We went into the kitchen, where Brother Frank shut the door and slid the heavy old bolt.

'Cup of tea,' he said, his brogue coming out again nice and strong. 'A nice cuppa. That's what you need.'

'I think I need something more than that,' I said.

He got up and put the kettle on the stove.

'Jane,' he said, 'I would normally have tried to do this in a much slower, more organic way — preferably over the course of several years, with a team of spiritual counselors and psychologists on standby. But there is no time now, so I have to be blunt, and you have to rearrange your concept of reality very quickly. For this, I apologize. But you must listen, and you must listen well.'

He dropped tea bags into some mugs with amazing calmness.

'Everything you have seen tonight is quite real. Everything you have seen over the last few days, and I have no doubt you have seen some interesting things, is quite real. You friend Allison made a compact with an emissary of what we sometimes refer to as Satan.'

'You're saying Lanalee is the devil?'

'It's complicated,' Owen said. 'People get it all mixed up. There is no one Satan. Satan is kind of like a corporation. It's made up of its members. Lanalee is a member.'

'A corporation? And Lanalee works for them?'

'She's...' Owen struggled for the words. 'She's like a really good intern who's definitely going to get a full-time job there. Demons are always moving up; new ones are always coming in. You always have to keep trying to get promoted.'

'Many large corporations are actually modeled on hell,' Brother Frank added. 'The policies and organization are almost identical. Hell, of course, is much worse. Sugar?'

'What?'

'In your tea?'

I nodded dumbly.

'When you make a contract with them,' Owen went on, 'one of two things happens. Either they simply suck you dry of energy and life force to keep themselves going, or they recruit you and you join the company. They decide which; you don't.'

'In your case, Jane,' Brother Frank said, setting a mug in front of me, 'I think they will probably try to recruit you. You would be demonized. You have intelligence, talents, strength. I have little doubt that you were always the target and that Allison was used to get to you.'

'Which is when I was sent,' Owen chimed in.

'By who?' I asked.

Brother Frank and Owen glanced at each other.

'We should just move on,' I said.

'We should,' Brother Frank agreed.

I drank the scalding tea. It burned my lips, but I didn't care.

'What happened between you and Lanalee?' Owen asked. 'We need to know.'

There was nothing else for it now. The story had to come out. They got the whole thing — the book, the dream, the contract, the works. They didn't say a word the entire time.

'Where did she mark you?' Owen asked when I was finished.

I grudgingly pulled up my sleeve. He took my arm in his frigid hands. He poked it roughly with his thumb, rubbing at it.

'That is not good,' he said. 'It's real. No question.'

There was a knock at the door. One of the brothers came in to get some hot chocolate, so we had to pretend that we were doing a math review session for a few minutes. I couldn't really get into it. I kept staring at the wall while Brother Frank talked about the wonders of parabolas. He promptly switched back as soon as the other brother was gone.

'The Poodle Club is not the only secret organization operating inside St. Teresa's,' he said. 'It's very much time that you understood this.'

'Oh?' I said, trying to sound calm.

'Along with being a brother of the Order of St. Sebastian, I am part of the order of St. Otto. We exist to fight demons and to hold back the presence of the Dark One.'

'You're... a *demon hunter*?'

'It's not really as exciting as it sounds,' he said. 'There is a surprising amount of paperwork involved. We are unknown to many members of the church. Only the highest echelons know of our existence. We have only one other member inside St. Teresa's.'

'Who?' I asked.

'Sister Charles,' he said.

'Shut up.'

177

'Sister Charles,' he said darkly, 'is twenty-eight years old. I recruited her personally six years ago.'

They watched me take in this news.

'She's one of the few people I've ever known who has repelled an advance from Lanalee. Sister Charles was a ballet dancer, you see. A very good one. She was poised for great success — and she was in fact offered this success by an agent. She was tempted but ultimately refused. In retaliation, Lanalee severed her toes.'

'Twenty-eight?'

'Lanalee sapped her life force. She literally consumed her youth. In one three-day span, I saw Sister Charles — who was then named Emma Bright — go from a muscular and vibrant dancer to an old woman. And she was lucky. Very lucky. She had been watching Lanalee very carefully. She knew, for instance, that Lanalee brought you and Allison to the chapel on the night that she had the Poodle display set up.'

'You knew that?'

'We also knew St. Sebastian's was an old Satanist property, of course. And it didn't take us long to figure out that it was connected to a very powerful force. But Lanalee's never actually turned up here before. She usually appears in big cities — New York, Boston, Vienna, London, Paris… But we knew it was only a matter of time before she returned here. One day before class started, her name simply appeared in the registration lists.'

'We don't have time to mess around,' Owen said. 'We have two days until Halloween, when the contract expires. This is not good news for you.'

'So what should I do?'

'We'll try to think of a way that the deal can be broken. Otherwise, go to school tomorrow, act as normally as you can. Let Lanalee think you're not even trying to do anything about this, like it doesn't scare you. It might increase the chance of her making a mistake.'

'And Jane,' Brother Frank added, 'don't go trying to fix this one on your own again. From now on, you're with us.'

Chapter 28

I didn't sleep. I didn't even think about sleeping. I dressed for school at four in the morning and startled my dad by being at the kitchen table long before he got downstairs.

At school, the halls were humming with a low-frequency jumpiness that I'd only felt one time when the Sebastian's guys came over to help move some desks. This feeling was even stronger. Girls were fingering their necks a lot. I noticed that a lot of people seemed to be wearing similar gold necklaces. Cassie walked by, furiously trying to balance her Filofax on a pile of books and write in it.

'Hey,' I called. 'Cass.'

She begrudgingly spared me a moment. She focused on my neck while I looked at hers. She was wearing a short gold choker with a poodle charm dangling from it.

'Where's yours?' she asked. 'Didn't you get one?'

'Sure,' I lied. 'I got one.'

'The note said we're supposed to wear it all the time,' she said. 'You should put it on. And God, did you get all those e-mails this morning? Alumni reps from every school

I'm applying to got in touch with me. This is so it, Jane. Harvard, Yale, Princeton. There was even one from Oxford! Did you get those?'

'Sure,' I lied again. 'And the Poodle Prom stuff. Where is it again?'

'The Biltmore Hotel ballroom. Tomorrow night at eight. Halloween. Jane, didn't' you read your note?'

'I was too busy with all those e-mails,' I said. 'Hardly any time to get ready for all this.'

'I know! I was supposed to take the SAT again on Saturday, but I'll just skip this time. I mean, I need a dress, a manicure, shoes... Pretty much everyone is going to blow off at some point today. A lot of people didn't come in. You better get started.'

'Right,' I said. 'Definitely.'

Sister Albert and Sister Charles were coming down the hall with a purposeful gait. Sister Rose Marie was trailing behind them, but I got the feeling that her presence wasn't official. I think she was following along like a demerit vulture, waiting for her chance to pounce.

'They must know,' Cassie said, buttoning up the collar of her shirt to hide the charm.

I stepped aside to watch and see where they were going and was surprised when they stopped directly in front of me.

'Miss Jarvis,' Sister Albert said. 'Please open your locker.'

When someone storms up to you like that and demands that you open your locker, the chances seem high that something in there is going to produce a very unwelcome surprise. And with Lanalee running around, that was no shock. But it wasn't Lanalee who came up and stood beside Sister.

It was Allison.

I noticed the roots were gone, and the little red hair helmet was looking more shiny than ever. She locked eyes with me, then lifted her chin just ever so slightly and ran her fingers along her neck, making sure I caught the faint glint of gold there.

'Now, Miss Jarvis,' Sister said. 'Don't try to stall.'

I looked at her blankly, shrugged, and turned and opened the lock. A crowd had gathered now. I could feel them at my back. I swung open the door. It looked like my locker, nothing out of the ordinary. A big mess of books and paper and Post-its.

I stepped aside so that Sister Albert could come over and see for herself. She reached in and poked around a bit. When that produced nothing, she took out books and shook out the pages. When she grabbed my Calculus II book, four red sparkling envelopes fluttered to the ground. Leafing through a notebook, she found a draft of the letter that had obviously come in the envelopes.

'I'm surprised, Miss Jarvis,' Sister said, bending to pick up the envelopes. 'I'm very surprised you kept any of these things here. You are much smarter than that. Maybe you weren't finished?'

'Those aren't mine,' I said. 'Someone put them in my locker. You're right. If I had been doing this, there's no way I would have kept the stuff here.'

And that's when Ally chimed in.

'She tried to get me to do it with her, Sister,' she said, turning a cold gaze on me. 'She said she hated it here. The Poodle Club thing was just the beginning.'

'*What?*' I said.

'I think you should wait in my office, Jane,' Sister Albert said.

'I will take her, Sister.'

It was Sister Charles, looping up behind me and catching me by the arm. She walked me halfway to the office before she spoke.

'You know who I am, I presume,' she said quietly.

'Brother Frank told me,' I said. 'What happens now?'

'You'll be expelled,' she said. 'I think there is little question of that.'

'Can't you do something? You know I didn't do it.'

'That is not important now.'

'Yes, it is!' I said. 'My whole life could change! I can't get kicked out of high school!'

'Jane,' she said, stopping and backing me up in the corner behind the statue of St. Sebastian, to the point where I nearly had a fake arrow in my eye. 'If you think for even one moment that is important now, we are sunk. We are now in the battle for eternal souls. There is only one way, Jane. You must give all but your soul. School is nothing. Your possessions are nothing. Your body is nothing. Your life is nothing. Toss these things away like garbage. But hold on to your soul.'

'It's a little late for that,' I said. 'Maybe you could have mentioned this in class?'

'It is *not* too late,' she snapped. Her eyes glowed under

her thin, bluish eyelids. Her pupils had gone milky, but I could see, looking at them at close range, that her gaze was still young and strong. Her skin was excessively wrinkled, but it still retained a faint hint of peachy youthfulness. It was like the ageing process had been started from the outside but hadn't penetrated the core.

'It's not?' I asked.

'It is never too late,' she said. 'Soul eaters are greedy, Jane, and the greedy make mistakes. As long as there is desire, there will be mistakes. Know that you are pure and know that you are fearless and you can make no mistakes. We will be in touch. Brother Frank or Owen will contact you, and I will continue to watch Lanalee.'

'Does she recognize you?' I asked.

'Oh yes,' she said. 'She certainly knows who I am. She takes great delight in what she did to me. But I know I am very fortunate. Now, Jane, is your hour to be everything you can possibly be. Now you must be your best, far beyond what you've ever imagined. This is your time, Jane.'

And with that, she gently took my arm again and led me to my academic doom.

Chapter 29

❦

There was no big judicial procedure involved in my expulsion. A private school like St. T.'s can throw you out at their discretion. They had a file drawer full of proof that I was a problem. They had physical evidence linking me to the Poodle Club. Case closed. My mother was called. My official St. Teresa's insignia was removed from my blazer with a small pair of scissors. Sister Rose Marie escorted me to my locker to clean it out. A crowd gathered and watched me. I was out on the new, smooth driveway within the hour, my belongings in shopping bags.

When my mother pulled up, she had only one question.

'Is this about Elton?' she asked.

Other than that, she was surprisingly quiet and thoughtful. I was permitted to go to my room while she spoke to my father. I waited all day to hear from Owen, but he never called. No one called. It was a silent wait. In the late afternoon, I was told we were going for dinner, but no explanation was given.

At least Joan was impressed.

'Were you really going to blow the place up?' she asked as she burst into my room after school.

'What?'

'I heard you wanted to blow up your school.'

'Who told you that?'

'I can't remember,' she said. Someone. You could probably build a bomb. You're good at stuff like that. Maybe Dad taught you.'

Every once in a while I get this paranoid idea that my sister is actually a genius and she says these king of things to test me.

'No, Joan. He didn't teach me how to build bombs. He just taught me to kill with my bare hands.'

'Or were you just going to burn it down?'

'I wasn't going to burn anything down or blow anything up,' I said. 'Have you met me?'

'You burned your book.'

Oh, right. There was the whole book-exploding thing. Points to Joan on that one.

'Is this about Elton?' she asked.

'Not *everything* is about Elton,' I said. 'Elton is not the center of the universe.'

'Sorry,' she said, flopping down on her bed. 'This is just so — not you. You've been acting weird. And now you've been kicked out of school. I don't understand.'

She flopped over on her back and gazed at me upside down.

'There's just something going on right now,' I said. 'There's a problem I have to solve, and once I do, everything will be fine.'

'What?'

'I can't tell you.'

'Why not?' She flipped over to her stomach. 'I can help. I want to help.'

She did want to help. Maybe in this new, rearranged universe I lived in, Joan was the smart one. There was no point in not letting her try. I hadn't exactly come up with anything.

'Okay,' I said. 'But you can't tell Mom or Dad.'

'I won't,' she said excitedly.

'What if you had to get into an event at the Biltmore Hotel, but you couldn't get an invitation. How would you do it?'

She buried her face into my bed and devoted herself to thought. After maybe five minutes of silence, her head jerked upright.

'I'd call Carbo and ask him to get me a job,' she said.

'Who is Carbo?'

'This guy who used to go to my school, Chris Carbolini. He runs part of the catering service now. He hires people all the time to do little jobs. He can probably get you in.'

'Joan… are you serious?'

'I can call Harvest, who can call Britney, and she can call Rina, who used to date Carbo's brother!'

Within minutes, the thing was done. I had an in at the Biltmore — and all because of Joan. There was a knock on my door. My mother stood there, smiling. Joan and I exchanged worried looks.

'You're father's home,' she said. 'We're going to go to Linda's for some pizza. Come on downstairs.'

This was a completely illogical turn of events. My parents had delayed their total menu breakdown and instead taken my to my favorite pizza place for dinner. This hardly seemed like a punishment. They even insisted that I got to pick everything and that I should order anything that looked good. We ended up with a massive Greek salad, garlic knots, a bowl of black olives, a four-cheese pizza with ham and pineapple, and another with artichokes and sausage.

'I did some research today,' my dad said, grabbing a slice of pizza and carefully picking off the pineapple. 'I let my TAs take over, and I talked to some people in the school of education. And now, we have some good news for you, Jane.'

'Obviously,' my mom cut in, 'we're not happy about the expulsion, but to be fair, St. Teresa's was never a good fit for you. We wanted to send you to a more specialized school, but it simply wasn't affordable.'

'But something's come up,' my dad went on. 'Have you ever heard of the Weddle Program?'

I shook my head.

'It's a new program for highly advanced learners in Boston. It's a self-paced, extremely innovative place. It's beautiful, Jane. The students live in two brownstone mansions, and you use classrooms at Boston University and MIT for your work. Here are some pictures and information.'

He pulled some printed-out web site pages from inside his coat. It was all that he had described — two long, copperly-colored buildings. A happy dorm room with half a dozen people crammed in, hanging out together. Glowing reports of academic freedom, the absence of useless rules and standards. Just a happy home for the smart and slightly ill-adjusted, smack in the middle of the biggest college town in the country. In short, paradise.

'They do one major field research trip a year,' he said. 'This year, they'll be going to do rain forest studies in Brazil.'

'You get kicked out of school, and you get to go to Brazil?' Joan asked. '*I* can get kicked out.'

'It's to do lab work, Joan,' my dad said kindly. 'They do biology and chemistry all day.'

'Oh. Never mind.'

'It's a great place, Jane,' my mother said, reaching for my hand. 'There are only thirty people in the whole program, all just as intelligent as you. We think this could be where you really belong. We'll be sad not to have you at home, but you'll be close. And you can come home for weekends in the spring if you want. And we can be there in an hour if you need us.'

'And there's one other thing,' my dad said. 'We got lucky. Purely by coincidence, they just got a late-filing grant to accept one more student, and as long as that student is in place by November first, it's fine. Which means that you'd have to leave tomorrow and get settled in and registered. In order to make up the time, you'd have to do class work on the weekends through December, but then you should be all caught up. But this grant will pay for the entire program. They'll give it to you, Jane, if you accept right now. Isn't that great!'

I picked all of the green olives off my pizza and set them to one side. Obviously, this was not a tricky choice. At least not on the surface. One option was a cutting-edge program in Boston that would salvage my whole future. The other option was… to do nothing. I only had a day. I needed that day.

'Can't they wait a day or two?' I asked.

'Why wait?' my dad said. 'The only other option is trying to get you into Joan's school, but you're already behind. This school will set things right, Jane. If you want to go to Harvard or Yale or MIT or wherever, this is where you need to go. They'll repair your record, and you'll meet and work with the right people. Frankly, this school is a miracle. What's there to think about? All you have to do is say yes now.'

I stared into the grotesque grin of the tiny carved pumpkin that glowed on our table. It was a miracle, all right. A perfect school, a grant at the last minute for the first student who came along. It was just the kind of thing that might happen to someone who — oh, I don't know — absentmindedly signed a contract with the devil.

I sifted through the pages again. This time, the name popped off one, as if it was bolded and three-dimensional:

Headmaster Lazarus Fields welcomes you to a community of truly unique learners.

'Oh my God,' I said out loud.

'It's great, huh?' my mom said cheerfully.

I looked across at my two beaming, well-meaning parents and my glistening-eyed, supportive sister... all of whom were delighted, albeit unintentionally, to be packing me off to Devil Prep.

'I need a day,' I said, my throat suddenly dry. 'It's all happening so fast.'

The delight faded from my parents' expressions, and my sister quickly turned her interest to identifying all four cheeses on the pizza in front of her.

'Jane,' my mother said firmly, 'we don't *have* a day. Trust me, we don't like the thought of you not living at home, but this is a one-in-a-million opportunity that just fell together at the right time. And it's you who got kicked out. We're trying to be positive about it — but this is *your* doing.'

'So what is it?' my father said.

I had no choice. I had to say something. And the smartest move seemed to be to say the thing that caused me the least trouble right now.

'Sure,' I said. 'Okay. I don't know what I was just thinking. You're right. It's perfect.'

The ride home was fairly joyous, considering. My mom started making a list of all the things I would need for my dorm room. My father tried to explain to Joan the difference between the American South and South America.

We all went to bed early in preparation for the day ahead, but I couldn't sleep. I couldn't go to Boston the next day. I couldn't go to this perfect, wonderful program that was waiting for me with open arms. No. I had to stay in Providence and fight the devil.

I paced.

At around two in the morning, as I went down to get what had to be my twentieth glass of juice, I was not surprised to look out the window and find Owen silently waiting in the cold.

Chapter 30

'I guess you heard the news,' I said.

I was sitting on my front porch, bundled in a bathrobe and my sister's silver ski jacket. Owen sat beside me in an oversized plaid lumberjack kind of coat, an obvious hand-me-down.

'We heard. Allison turned on you. Not to depress you, but that's not shocking.'

'Yup. And magically, the perfect school in Boston decided to let me in. They just happened to get a grant *today*, which they need to use by *tomorrow*. Which is when I'm supposed to leave.'

'Tomorrow? You can't go tomorrow.'

'I know that,' I said. 'I have to wash dishes for a guy named Carbo tomorrow. Somehow, though, I don't think my parents are going to accept that. We're supposed to be packing my things in the morning. Oh, and Lazarus Fields is the headmaster. You have a plan, right?'

'Working on it.'

Even though my coat was warmer, he reached over and rubbed my arm hard to get the circulation going.

'Can I ask you a personal question?' I said.

'What?'

'How did it happen?'

'How did what happen?'

'How did you... you know?'

'What?'

'Die,' I finally said. 'How did you die?'

'Oh, that. Accident.'

'What kind of accident?'

'I worked for a greengrocer,' he said. 'Mr. Bioni. He wasn't a really friendly guy. He used to make me sleep in the store to take early morning deliveries. He would lock me in because he thought that would keep me from stealing his things — not that I ever did. I worked really hard for him. My family needed the money. I was sort of the main support. My dad was sick and couldn't work. So I was there, sleeping, when a huge fire broke out at the bakery next door. The flames went right through the wall. I couldn't get out. That was pretty much that.'

'That's horrible,' I said. 'Lanalee said something about you knowing about fire.'

'Oh yeah,' he said dismissively. 'She would. It's been a while. It doesn't bother me anymore. I think my death was even mentioned in a book on reforming working conditions in the early twentieth century.'

'The what?' I asked. 'When was this?'

'1904.'

'You're over a hundred years old?'

'Yeah.'

'How old were you when you died?'

'Same age I am now,' he said. 'Fourteen.'

'You died when you were fourteen? At *work*?'

'It doesn't matter how old you are,' he said. 'Age is a human thing. It's kind of meaningless, something people get hung up on, like clothes or something.'

'But you died kind of... prematurely.'

'There is no dying prematurely,' he said. 'Whenever you die, that's the right time for you. Maybe your time is when you're three, maybe it's when you're a hundred and three.'

'So, Lanalee's dead too?'

'Yeah, but she died old. Really old. I think she was ninety-five or something. The evil live a long time. They tend to be good at stuff — making money, taking care of themselves. They don't usually get stuck in fires at locked grocery stores.'

He was trying to keep his voice level, but it gave way a bit. There was resentment there.

'But she looks young.'

'She took that body from a girl in France, maybe a year ago. See, they take things to help themselves. They take souls, bodies — they take whatever they need or want to sustain themselves. They're like parasites. Sure, maybe they'll give you some stuff to get you to sign, but they always do it for themselves.'

'So, what do you do it for?'

'I like to make things right,' he said. 'I like to take care of people.'

He paused a minute.

'Allison sold out today,' he said.

'Good to know you were paying attention.'

'There can only be one reason for that,' he said. 'The stakes must have changed again.'

'What?'

'A deal,' he said simply. 'Lanalee's done another deal.'

Chapter 31

It was about three in the morning as we approached the Tremone house.

She came to the door in a pair of red Chinese silk pajamas. A fuzzy red eye-cover embroidered with the words *The bitch is sleeping* was pulled back over her forehead.

'Oh,' she said. 'It's you. I don't hold court at this hour usually, but seeing it's a special day, I'll make an exception. Come on. And bring Owen. I'm sure he's lurking around out there somewhere.'

I went back down the steps, over to the tree that Owen was, in fact, lurking behind.

'She says you can come in,' I said.

'No thanks. I'll stay out here. We're not really supposed to mingle — it confuses things. Find out what happened and leave. No dealing.'

'I know.'

'Seriously, Jane. No dealing.'

'Okay,' I said. 'Okay.'

197

I went back up to the door, where Lanalee was drooping sleepily.

'He doesn't want to come in,' I said.

'Yeah, Owen kind of likes the cold,' she said. 'He hasn't had much luck with hot places. Well, then, princess, you'd better follow me.'

Even though no one was in the room, the downstairs fireplace was going strong, and all of the lights were on.

'David!' Lanalee screamed.

A thing — a person — came down the stairs, wrapped in a plush red bath wrap. I barely recognized him. He was obviously cold, shivering visibly, and pruned to the point where he looked like he was about a hundred. Only his shoe-polish black hair and doe-like eyes were the same.

'Have you been in the bath all this time?' I asked.

'I forgot about him,' Lanalee said, twisting her face into a smile. 'I never told him to come out.'

David gripped the rail and sneezed with such force I thought he'd broken a rib.

'David, refreshments for us, please. Maybe some cocoa with those little homemade pink marshmallows. I got the best marshmallows at Trader Joe's!'

She said this last thing to me, excitedly, as if I'd just stopped over in my robe and slippers in the middle of the night to see if she had any good snacks. David came down the stairs, gripping the rail fiercely. I could see his pale legs now, bloated and purplish from being in bathwater for days. He seemed barely able to walk. He went through the archways to the kitchen.

'Seriously,' she said. 'They're square and pink, and

they're handmade by these farmers or something. They are *too* good.'

'We need to talk,' I said.

'Oh, I know why you're here,' she said with a smile. 'You're here because you're not stupid.'

She got up and went over to a long shelf mostly full of anatomy textbooks and art books. The bottom shelf had a few leather-bound albums. She pulled out one of these, a cracked red one.

'This is the Codex,' she said. 'This is the record of all the disagreements I make.'

'Disagreements?'

'I don't like to call them agreements. It's too positive.'

'Disagreements? You seem like more of a poser than any poser I've met.'

She smiled faintly and opened it. After flipping through a few pages, which I could clearly see were class notes and homework assignments, she found what she was looking for.

'Here,' she said, passing me the book. 'Read it yourself.' I did. It read:

You, Allison Francis Concord, have entered into an official contract with a representative of the Satanic High Command, Hearth of the Cold and All-Consuming Fire, Destroyer of Worlds, Consumer of Souls, Taker of the Life Breath, Guardian of the Bottomless Ocean of Sorrow, Bearer of the Lance of Endless Pain, Lanalee Tremone, 10B. *Whereby, you agree*

that you will receive the bounty and comfort you
desire and the worldly leadership of the Poodle
Club, in exchange for the soul of one Jane
Elizabeth Jarvis, which you will secure by ensuring
that the quarry (JEJ)

'I'm quarry?' I asked.
Lanalee grinned.

...will be thwarted in her attempt to receive
a kiss from one Andrew Elton on All Hallows'
Eve. Should you fail in this, you will surrender
your soul in her stead.

David returned in the interim, with a massive mug of
cocoa that Lanalee greedily grabbed. She shoved the Codex
into his chest, and he dutifully staggered over to the
bookshelf to replace it.

All I could think to say was, 'Why?'

She laughed so hard that she had to squeeze her nose
to keep cocoa from coming out. David laughed as well,
out of obligation.

'Ow,' she said. 'Hotness on the nasal membrane. Why?
Okay. Let me give you a for instance. You know how you
watch television sometimes and you see some new
somebody or other? Usually blond, usually skinny, usually
very talentless, often in synthetic fibers? These people can't
really sing, are too stupid to know their own names —
they just have a catchy song and some really good eyeliner?
And you ask yourself, not unreasonably, *how*? How did

this happen? How could some no-talent idiot get a big record contract, make big dance music videos, rise up overnight?'

She got up and went over to finger-dust her perfume bottles. David sat on the floor near our feet and watched her admiringly.

'It happens because *we do it*, Jane. I can do a celebrity conversion in less time than it takes me to get a pedicure.'

'Mistress is so good at this stuff,' David said, hugging his robe tight around his purple legs.

'All it takes is a few phone calls to some friends,' Lanalee said. 'And it's very, very hard to go back when you've had a taste.'

'It's true,' David said, nodding sagely. 'So true.'

'David, shut up and get Jane some cocoa. She hasn't tried my pink marshmallows.'

David unwillingly left his spot by the fire. Lanalee came and sat next to me, adjusting Joan's ski jacket so that it sat more easily over my fluffy robe.

'Allison didn't want to lose what I had given her,' she went on. 'So she came back and asked me to give her everything, and in return, she would simply make sure you lost. I get you. She gets stuff. Simple. Beautiful. And just plain wrong. And really, more than I expected from her. I *like* that girl now! I'd still rather have you, though. I'm glad we're taking care of that.'

David returned with another cup, which Lanalee took as he was passing it to me.

'So, is that what you wanted to know?' she asked.

'Yes,' I said, feeling a churning pain in my stomach.

I had put myself on the line to save Allison, and she had turned on me. My best friend.

'Great.' Lanalee downed the cocoa in one gulp and stood. 'Well, I'm awake now. Want to make some pancakes or something?'

'No, I just want to go.'

'Whatever you want. You know where the door is. See you in hell!'

Owen Secret-Serviced himself out from behind the tree as I came down the steps. I sank down on the last one and put my head in my hands.

'What happened?' he asked, coming and standing over me.

'You were right,' I said. 'Ally went back. She did another deal. And she's going to make sure I lose.'

I wrapped my arms completely around my head and tried to see if I could squeeze myself out of consciousness. It didn't work. Owen didn't sit down. He just continued to stand there, looking down at me.

'There's only one thing you can do,' he said.

I squeezed my head some more.

'Are you listening?'

'No.'

'In sixteen hours, you have to win this bet.'

'And send my best friend to wherever it is that Lanalee comes from? Hell?'

'That's right.'

When I peered up from the folds of my own arms, I noticed what seemed like a thousand tiny gold dabs of light all around us. They were under parked cars. On porches. Across the street. In the bushes.

'What,' I asked slowly, 'are those?'

He turned and looked.

'Cats,' he said.

'Cats?'

Now that he said it, I could make out tiny shadowy forms, crouching low, pacing slowly.

'What are they doing?'

'Watching the house.'

'Why?'

'Because they know something is wrong. Cats are good guards. They can feel the time is coming.'

'There were cats on my porch the other night.'

'They were probably trying to protect your house. They can't do much, but it's in their nature to try. So *get up*, Jane.'

'And go where?'

'Come with me. There's no time for you to go home. You can't go back. Not right now. You know that.'

So that, in short, is how I ended up running away from home on the night of my high school expulsion.

Chapter 32

Owen led me up a narrow, very steep staircase, past three bedrooms, to an even tinier staircase. The floorboards creaked so loudly that it sounded like the house was about to implode into a shower of matchstick-sized pieces, but no one stirred.

It's always interesting to have a look in people's bedrooms. It can tell you a lot. Owen's room took up the entire third floor, but it was hardly spacious; the ceiling came to just an inch or two above his head. There was an old dresser with the knobs hanging a bit loose. There was a switched-off electrical heater, so it was absolutely frigid.

'You can sleep in my bed,' Owen said.

'Your bed?'

'I'm not sleeping tonight,' he said quickly. 'I'm not saying we're going to share.'

I walked over to a desk with a neat stack of notebooks and textbooks on top. On the shelf above, there was a perfectly organized row of books. I walked over and read the spines — they were all old books, in some cases held together with carefully placed pieces of yellowed tape. Most of them were adventure novels — *20,000 Leagues Under the Sea*, *Treasure Island*, *The Time Machine*, *Around the World in 80 Days*. There were others as well, larger books with titles like *The Modern World* and *The Future of Flight*. I reached for one of those but stopped when I noticed that Owen had frozen with an armload of folded blankets that he had just removed from his closet.

'Sorry,' I said.

'It's okay. Just… be careful. They're kind of fragile.'

I took down *The Modern World* and opened it gingerly. The pages were strong and shiny despite their age. I looked over the drawings of 'modern' cities, with strange lemon-shaped flying machines attaching themselves to the tops of skyscrapers.

'You like classics,' I said. 'They are all pretty old books. Are you some kind of collector?'

'They were all mine,' he said, resuming movement but still watching me out of the corner of his eye.

This stopped me cold. I closed the book with excessive caution and slid it back into place on the shelf. Owen visibly relaxed a bit, but then turned a wary glance to the heater.

'I guess if you're sleeping here, I should turn that on,' he said.

'Don't you usually?'

'These things are fire risks,' he said, bending over and examining the cord.

'So how do you sleep? It's freezing in here.'

'I dress warm. Anyway, I'll be awake tonight.'

He switched on the heater and squared himself off in a chair just opposite it.

I pulled off the coat and got into Owen's bed. It may have looked like a military cot, but it felt like the warmest, most welcoming refuge on earth. I looked up to see Owen's gaze fixed on me, his fine eyebrows set in a straight line. Then I went to sleep.

I woke up with a snort and a start. Owen was wide awake, standing at the window. I automatically reached up and gave my spikes a tufting and rubbed my face. He didn't seem to notice how I looked.

'Morning,' he said gruffly. 'You should go down and get some breakfast.'

'Don't you want any?'

'I think better on an empty stomach,' he said. 'Go downstairs and eat. Brother Frank is waiting for you.'

'Did you have any good ideas overnight?'

'I'm working on it. Go eat. You need to have lots of energy today, so don't be all girly and say you aren't hungry.'

I ignored the girly remark.

Brother Frank was sitting at the kitchen table, nursing a cup of coffee. The oak outside the window was completely naked except for a few straggling dead leaves that had survived the last few weeks, clinging to the branches like those kittens in the Hang in There! posters. The sky was an unpromising steel gray.

'Jane,' he said, perking up at my appearance. 'Good morning. Let's have some breakfast.'

He proceeded to make me a breakfast that could easily have fed eight — pancakes, toast, a leftover cinnamon roll, bacon, fruit salad. When it was all on the table, I picked at a pancake and he pushed around a piece of bacon, but really, neither of us ate much.

'Okay,' I said, 'just tell me. What does it mean?'

He knew what I was asking. I was asking, *What does it mean to sell your soul?*

'Do you really want to know?'

'I think I should,' I said. 'Knowledge is power, right?'

'That point is debatable.'

'Come on,' I said. 'There has to be a perk to this. Do I get any cool abilities? Will I be able to breathe fire or anything? I mean, Lanalee seems to like being a demon.'

'I suppose demons have a place in our world,' he said thoughtfully. 'In a sense, they actually help get things done because good things often come from bad. In this world, we have to have both. They balance each other out.'

'So it's not *all* bad.'

He rubbed his forehead and pushed the plate toward me.

'Here,' he said, 'have another pancake.'

We ate in silence until I worked up enough courage to speak again.

'How do you know Owen?' I asked.

'He's lived with our order since the early 1900s,' he said. 'Not just here — in various locations. Every few years or so, one of the brothers or sisters who works in a hospital arranges to get him a new birth certificate. Otherwise, it's hard to explain someone who's been fourteen years old for as long as anyone can remember.'

'You'd think they'd send someone... older,' I said.

'Don't underestimate Owen.'

Outside, some little kids were off to school in their costumes. Among them, there were tiny devils in red pajamas carrying plastic pitchforks.

'Maybe it won't be too bad,' I said. 'Maybe it will be like that.'

He put his hand over mine.

'You'll never find out,' he said. 'I believe that. They've taken a lot of people, but they can't have you.'

Chapter 33

I knew my parents had to be beside themselves with worry. I'd been kicked out of school and then disappeared from my bed in the middle of the night. I had to call them. But my parents were smart people — they could trace the number that came up on the caller ID. So I shuffled out of Brother Frank's house into the cold morning to find a pay phone. I knew there was one on Thayer Street, but that was too common a thoroughfare and was a direct line to Brown, so I could have easily bumped into my dad. That wouldn't work.

I opted instead to walk toward the Rhode Island School of Design, Providence's other big school. This had several advantages. There was likely to be a phone around somewhere, I didn't know anyone who would be going that way, and art students were a lot less likely to notice a very small girl dressed up in hand-me-down guys' clothes, several sizes too large.

This worked well. I found a fairly secluded phone behind the student center, and with my scruffy spikes and hobo wear, I fitted right in with the stream of art students making their bleary way to class, dragging massive portfolios and art boxes. When I reached for the phone, my arm disappeared up the long sleeve. I looked like I was trying to do a magic trick where I was trying to slip my way out of a massive sack while handcuffed. It was not graceful.

Joan picked up the phone on the first ring.

'Joan,' I said quickly. 'I'm fine. Don't say anything about the Biltmore.'

'Oh my God, Jane! Where are you?'

My mother was on the line in the next instant, demanding everything a panicked parent demands in situations like this. Where was I? Was I okay? Was I coming home? Was I upset about the school in Boston? Was I with Allison?

I almost laughed at that last one.

'I just need a day,' I said.

'Jane...'

There was so much worry and love in her voice that I felt a physical pang — a kind of broken-guitar-string plunk. This was likely to be one of the last times I ever spoke to my mother. Then I would be gone. How I would go, I had no idea. Maybe tomorrow they would find a body — maybe I would just vanish...There would be questions forever, and they would never know that the reality was worse than even their very worst nightmares.

And I would never see them again. Joan would never ask me if Canada was in South America; Crick would never try to wake me up by chewing at the fringe of my bedspread. I would never see my mother, tousle-haired at noon, coming downstairs and telling us about the nightly adventures she had with the head chef of the restaurant. My dad would never push over his Sudoku and ask for my help, which he never needed. He just always liked to show me how much he thought of my abilities. My father loved me. And I loved them. And now I was hurting them, and the pay phone clamped to my ear was cold. My world was over. Jane Jarvis was coming to an end. A very bad end.

I set my teeth hard and steadied myself. I could not give in to those thoughts.

'You have to trust me,' I said quickly. 'I need this day, more than I've ever needed any day in my life.'

I pushed on when she tried to speak.

'Please,' I said. 'Trust me. I am fine. I love you. Okay? I have to go now.'

I clapped the phone back onto the hook with too much force. It must have sounded like an angry, crazed hang-up. I stood there, my hand still on it, as if trying to soften the blow after the fact. Then I let go, pulling one finger loose at a time, and made my way slowly back to Brother Frank's.

Owen was sitting in the living room, cross-legged in the middle of the floor, poking at a gap between the floorboards with his fingernail.

'Where have *you* been?' he greeted me, jumping to his feet and coming over to me. He grabbed me by the shoulders, as if checking that I was actually there and wasn't just a walking pile of laundry.

'Calling my parents.'

'What?' He stepped back, and his face contorted in panic. 'You didn't tell them where you are, did you? They'll come for you. They'll try to take you…'

'I'm not stupid, Owen,' I said. 'No. I didn't tell them.'

I brushed past him and threw myself into a chair near the space heater. I stared into the glowing orange coils inside the metal casing. It was like hell was already everywhere.

'Brother Frank's out sending a message to the order,' he said briskly. 'We need to get to work. We lost time this morning while you were out.'

He said it in just a slightly accusatory way, as if instead of calling my parents to assure them that I was alive, I'd gone and gotten a manicure.

'Look, don't you have a weapon or something?' I asked. 'Some kind of magic water or something for fighting demons?'

'It's not *Lord of the Rings*,' he said. 'Do you think things really work like that?'

'Well, I didn't think there were angels or demon hunters, either,' I said. 'So forgive me for thinking you might have something useful, like the pointy stick of righteousness.'

'The pointy stick probably wouldn't do much good,' he said. 'It's not like you can kill her.'

Kill her. Why hadn't this occurred to me before. Why had it never crossed my mind to just kill her?

'Why not?' I asked. 'Why *can't* I just kill her? Why can't you just kill her?'

He shook his head.

'I can't kill her and she can't kill me because our sides have an agreement. We never directly get involved with each other. We're like two countries with a border that we agree on. The battle is all about human souls. They want to consume them. We want to protect them. Those are the rules between us.'

'But what about me?' I asked. 'I don't have those rules.'

'You could try to kill her body, but that would be bad.'

'Why is that bad?' I asked. 'Why is killing the demon not something we want to do?'

Owen shook his head.

'There's a demon expression — you go for the pearl, but you get the oyster shell too. The soul is the pearl, and the oyster shell is what it comes in, the body. Lanalee can only have one body at a time, but she can switch as many times as she likes. As long as she's bought the soul, the body is hers. If you killed Lanalee, she could go right into your body. Up until midnight tonight, she has a valid contract on you. You'd lose instantly. Also, killing is wrong. Even killing demons.'

'So we're back to the contract.'

'Right,' Owen said with a note of disgust. 'I can't believe this ends with kissing. I hate Lanalee... as much as I can hate anybody. Which I can't, really. Which sucks. She's doing this to get at me... I know it.'

'You think this is about *you*?' I said irritably.

'I'm not saying it's all about me. I'm just saying the

kissing part is to get at me. She's always trying to get at me. What does she mean by *kissing*?'

He punched his fist into the air a few times for no clear reason. He looked so bothered by it that I felt sorry for him.

'I think she means kissing,' I said.

'But what does that mean? What's the legal definition?'

'Is there a legal definition?'

'Well, it has to vary a little, right?' He ran his hand through his hair. 'From culture to culture? Like, there's French kissing...'

'She didn't specify tongue,' I said. 'And the physical specifications don't matter. It's the motivation, and that we'll never figure out.'

'We could dare him,' he said. 'Maybe he would do it as a dare.'

'Oh, thanks.'

'I'm just trying to think.'

'You can talk about it all day, but you're not Elton, so you don't know what it would take to want to kiss me.'

'Are you saying I don't want to kiss you?' he asked. 'I am a guy, no matter what it seems like.'

'No,' I said. 'I didn't mean anything by it.'

'Yes, you did,' he said plainly. 'You wanted me to say that I would know exactly what it would take to want to kiss you. In fact...'

'In fact, nothing,' I said.

'I can't kiss you,' he said.

'What do you mean, can't? And I don't want you to.'

An icy feeling had come over me. I had wanted him to. I'd wanted him to grab me and start making out with me wildly. I had no idea where the impulse had come from, but I was mortified that he had known it was there.

'There are rules,' he said. 'We can't get involved.'

'Owen,' I lied, 'I did *not* want you to kiss me.'

'Why do you just say the opposite of whatever someone else is saying?' he said. 'Do you just have to be difficult?'

'No. I just want to be clear.' Why was I lying? Why did I feel like I was on the verge of tears? Why was I having this fight when I should have been working feverishly on the problem?

'You're lying,' he said. 'You can't lie now, Jane. You have to tell the truth.'

'I am not lying.'

'Yes, you are,' he said. 'I'm over a hundred years old. I know things.'

'And stop saying that!' I said. 'You don't know. You're as clueless as anyone I've ever met.'

'Why won't you just admit it?' he said.

'Admit what? That you're clueless? Fine! You're clueless. How do I know this? Well, Mr. 116, we've been working on this problem for a while now and have come up with nothing. You can't save me.'

Owen looked stung.

'The day's not over,' he said. 'You should get yourself ready. I'll keep working.'

Chapter 34

While he was out, Brother Frank had gotten the 'black and whites' I needed for the event. He returned to the house with a pair of the most shapeless black pants I'd ever seen, but they fit me. The shirt was oversized and puffed out when I tried to tuck it in, as I was told I had to. The overall effect was a little less dressy, a little more pirate-y than I had hoped for.

Touchingly, he'd also made an attempt to get me makeup, so I was given a bag of bright red lipsticks, blue eye shadows, an under-eye cover, cotton-candy-pink blush, and what he probably thought was mascara, but was actually purple liquid eyeliner. I did the best I could with this, but I just ended up looking like a stripper dressed as a pirate. I washed my face and went back to zero.

There I was, reflected in all my glory. Short, badly dressed, with a face rubbed half raw. Blond hair looking a bit drier than normal.

The afternoon at the house was passed in near-total silence. Brother Frank sat on one side of the living room and Owen sat on the other. They occasionally asked each other questions like, 'What does act two-twenty say about holy water?' and, 'Do you think we could pull the Verona classic?' I was of no use at all.

When it was time to go, Owen came with me. Brother Frank gave me a tight hug.

'Keep strong,' he said. 'I'm going to meet with other members of the order. We have six hours, Jane. That's a long time.'

Lanalee was sitting in the lobby of the Biltmore, looking right at home with the opulent leathers and Oriental rugs. She had perched herself on a fat sofa and was popping candy corns from a bag.

As I approached, she waved us over.

'Fantastic outfit, Spike! I adore it. Is it Versace? Stella McCartney? Goodwill? Salvation Army?'

'It's called catering,' I said.

'Good for you. I knew you'd make it. That's why you're my champ. Hey, Owen. Can I have a few minutes with Jane?'

'No way,' he said.

'I'm not going to *do* anything to her,' she said. 'Maybe we can work something out.'

He looked at her with unveiled disgust.

'Not a chance.'

'Being fourteen and girl-less all these years has made you *so* uptight.' She sighed. 'Didn't you make any nice nookie with Jane? Oh, guess not. Rules are rules. Sorry I signed such a sexy little mama for my mark. Must have been hard for you to resist the temptation. I never resist temptation. That's why I always have such good skin, no matter what body I'm wearing. I'm full of happiness hormones. You must be full of hormones too...'

'Shut up, Lanalee,' he said stiffly.

'Nice place, huh?' Lanalee looked around fondly. 'I used to come here every once in a while when this place was new. That's why I suggested it. Actually, during the big stock market crash, you know, 1929, one of my guys jumped off the roof here.'

'So,' I said, 'who's coming to this? Who was asked?'

'Lots of people,' she said. 'Everyone with potential. I like to start things right. It's going to be a big party. The start of something big — and it all starts with you.'

She reached into her purse and removed the heart-shaped perfume bottle.

'It'll be fun,' she said. 'Think of it this way — it's like you're going to be a genie. You just never come out. This is nice perfume, too. There has to be a little still in there. You'll get to know the smell, I guess.'

She took off the stopper, sniffed a little, then replaced it and nodded.

'There's a little left. I bought this at Macy's in New York around then. I think 1934. But I've got lots of bottles. The oldest is one from when I was little. It's from 1838. I have a cocktail waitress in there. I made her into a Broadway star. I thought she deserved a special bottle since she was a celebrity. But this one — this was always my favorite. That's why I kept it for last. See? I really like you!'

She was obviously doing this I'm-two-hundred-years-old-and-I-keep-people-in-bottles thing to freak me out. To be honest, it was working.

I steeled myself by staring at the large flat-screen monitor that showed all the flight times in and out of the Providence airport. That was my reality — the one with airplanes and computer screens and things like that. At least it was for five more hours. And then I was going to squeeze into a purple bottle for all eternity.

'You aren't going to be so smug later,' Owen said.

'Oh, shut up.' Lanalee picked though her candy. 'You couldn't make your way out of a locked grocery store, so you're definitely not going to squeeze out of a binding contract. So spare me the alpha male. You may, however, have a piece of my delicious candy corn. I can't get enough of the stuff. It's just sugar and artificial coloring — my favorite foods.'

Lanalee held out a handful of candy. Owen stiffened a bit at the remark about the grocery store but didn't budge from his spot on the edge of the carpet.

'Oh, look!' she cooed. 'My favorite girl is here. Now we can really get started.'

I caught Allison's reflection in a mirror over the fireplace, and I didn't really want to turn to get the full effect. But Elton was with her, so I had to show a good face. She looked better than any human outside of a spy film should. Her dress was a flawless black satin, not so much fitted as spun around her — with a fine webbing of black netting around her shoulders. She wore a black velvet choker with a single red stone in the middle. And there was Elton, in a charcoal pin-striped suit and a cream-colored shirt. He nodded to me and looked down at the floor, away from my catering uniform.

'We should go up,' he said.

'Go ahead,' Lanalee said. 'I'm right behind you!'

I didn't so much as get a backward glance.

'I don't want to make you late, Jane,' Lanalee said, getting up. 'I'm sure you have things to do. Napkins to fold and spoons to polish. Better hurry or they might not let you stay!'

'Come on,' Owen said. 'Don't let her get to you. She's just trying to distract you so you can't think clearly. Ignore her.'

'She's hard to ignore.'

'You learn,' he said. 'Over time. You learn.'

Chapter 35

I arrived upstairs through a series of stark, padded elevators and dim stairwells, finally reaching the very top floor. I managed to check in with Carbo. He was easy enough to find. Joan told me that he was six-foot five and had a shaved head. I was given a water pitcher. Water glass filling was my duty for the night. I set the pitcher down the moment I went through the kitchen doors into the grand ballroom, and I didn't touch it again.

It was a remarkable sight. This was the highest floor, overlooking all of Providence. Security was tight, so Owen came up as well but didn't go into the ballroom. He stayed outside in the hallway. Invitations were scrutinized at the door by a massive woman in a blue sequined gown. She held them up to a candlelight and scratched at them with her nails. A few people tried to get in with fake ones. The woman spotted these instantly and snapped her fingers, two thick guys folded in from either side of the door, and the pretenders scrambled.

The room was lit entirely by candles, and there was

a guy (not a staff member) dressed in an old footman's outfit with a powdered wig who watched over them with a long snuffer on a pole. Every table was draped in deep maroon cloths, and each place was set with fine, intricately patterned silver. Several dozen flower arrangements were situated around the room — bundles of lilies and silver-white roses. A chef grilled up blood-rare steaks. A massive ice sculpture of a poodle stood in the center of a table heavily laden with hundreds and hundreds of delicately frosted cupcakes.

Mingling with the group of St. Teresa's kids and Sebastianites were maybe two dozen other people. I recognized many of them from my strange dream. Here they were, in the flesh, just as languid and gorgeous. His Assyrian Majesty was there, dressed in a long black robe with heavy lapis accessories. He was keeping to himself in the corner, quietly mumbling and poking his ringed finger into his drink. The others were much more social. None of them seemed to find it strange in the least that they were at some kind of high school prom, and they spread themselves through the crowd freely. David, dressed in a red smoking jacket, was poured over three plush chairs, completely prone. Several large poodles had free run of the place but most of the time were napping on massive velvet cushions under the window.

And, of course, my old friend Mr. Fields was there. He was dressed in a tuxedo with tails, a white tie, and a top hat.

'Jane!' he said, running up to me. 'You shouldn't be here. You should be getting settled in your room at school.

But this can't really be missed, can it? It's marvelous, isn't it? Everyone's here! And you look wonderful, I might add.'

An obvious lie, but he seemed to mean it. He was a friendly demon.

'Claris has been talking about you without pause,' he said. 'You must come over and say hello.'

'Maybe later,' I said. 'I'm working.'

The A3 strutted in side by side, and Lanalee welcomed them with open arms and swiftly guided them to a corner where they were warmly greeted by a group of tall women in red bodysuits who I vaguely recognized as being some English pop group. They seemed utterly at ease with Lanalee, awed by their surroundings.

It was amazing to me just how little time it took for my classmates to get used to my new role. Few of them even noticed me in my misshapen uniform. I was just there, like the chairs or the wall.

Well, except for Allison and Owen. They looked at me constantly. Elton didn't look over at all. It didn't help that Allison kept dragging him up to do every single dance. She made him dance the time warp. If I didn't believe the demonic thing before then, I believed it after seeing her prodding Elton to jump to the left and step to the right... the whole thing.

In my hell, there would be much time warping. We would probably do it before breakfast.

At eleven, when the dinner had been cleared away, there was a loud popping of corks. Then, with a bang and a loud cheer, a banner was dropped down from the magnificent ceiling that read: YOU HAVE BEEN ASKED. And the person holding the velvet rope that released the sign? Allison — looking magnificent and surrounded by an applauding and approving crowd of both friends and strangers.

I rejoined Owen in the hallway. He was staring out the window, down the side of the building, to the street below.

'Just say it again,' he said, pressing his forehead against the window. 'What was the bet?'

'I've told you. She said that Elton has to give me a kiss. It has to be Elton who gives it to me. I can't jump on him or anything.'

Many stories below us, costumed adults were making their way to parties in town. 'Paradise by the Dashboard Light' came thundering from inside the ballroom.

'DJs are from the other side,' I said. 'Right?'

'Yeah, a lot of them are,' he said. 'Especially the ones who do proms and weddings. How'd you know?'

'Just a guess. Anyone who tries to force other people into having fun like that... has to be evil.'

'It's an entry-level position.'

I turned to the window and watched the grown-up trick-or-treaters with him. A pack of adults staggered along, all in rabbit costumes.

'I'll miss this place,' I said. 'I'll bet people don't dress like rabbits in hell. Or maybe they do. Maybe we'll have to.'

'Don't talk like that.'

'Let's just admit it. I lost. Don't worry about it. You tried.'

'Stop it. I have to think. I just have to think. I'll be back.'

He walked away, gripping his head. I went back inside to circle the room. Lanalee drew herself away from the snacks to join me.

'It's pathetic that you're working here,' she said, offering me a cupcake, which I waved away.

'We do what we have to.'

'I know *why* you're doing it,' she said. 'I just don't like to see you serving anyone. Let me explain something to you. Some people are strong, and some people are weak. Some people are smart, and some people are stupid. Doesn't it make sense that the strong and the smart should control the stupid and the weak? The stupid and the weak work and make us things, buy what we sell them, believe the things we tell them. Why shouldn't it be that way?'

'You're saying some people are useless?' I asked.

'Not useless,' she said. 'Usually good for work. But useless for anything else. And don't give me that crap about everyone being special. Everyone is not special. Special means different, unique, a standout. Allison certainly wasn't special. She was just sappy and needy. And look what I did for *her*!'

We looked out at the dance floor, where Allison was pushing Elton through a line dance.

'It's almost hard to watch,' she said. 'I admit it. I can undo it all, though. I can turn him right back to you. I can give you everything you want. Look at my lovely friends. Powerful bankers and politicians. Musicians. Painters. Writers. Inventors. *These* are the people you belong with, Jane. I'll give you a real deal — not like the one I gave Allison. We have lots of places for someone like you back at home. See, home is a lot like high school — the smart, the popular, the powerful thrive. Having the right friends gets you everywhere.'

'God, you make it sound so tempting, Lanalee,' I said. 'Eternal high school. Sign me up.'

'Don't get snooty and righteous. Don't turn down something you haven't really felt. You got a tiny, tiny taste of it. You have no idea what I can give you. *No idea.* Come on, Jane. Don't be an idiot.'

'So, what are you suggesting?'

'Say you'll come with me now and there's no bottle for you. At midnight, I'll give you everything you could possibly want. We'll leave! We'll go to the airport and get on a plane. Where do you feel like going? London? Rome? Tokyo? We're there. We'll check into a five-star hotel, have them send up lobsters and champagne and piles of cake and we'll do this right. Just stop this sad little effort. You can't win.'

This was it — the knife's edge. I was hers anyway. We had no plan. I had no hope. If I went along with her, I'd at least get something out of the deal.

I remembered Sister Charles's words… give it all away, but hold on to your soul. Right now, it was hard. But there was a reality in that, a reality in Owen and Brother Frank, that I didn't see in this room.

'Cam I have that cupcake?' I asked.

'Of course!'

She handed it over.

'You do have good cupcakes,' I said, examining the high, creamy frosting.

'I only buy the best, sweetheart.'

'There's one thing, though.'

'What's that?' she asked.

'Not everything can be bought.'

With that, I jammed the thing into her face and walked across the suddenly silent room and out the door into the hallway. If I was going down, I was going down like that. Like Jane Jarvis. I had a reputation to uphold, after all.

Chapter 36

E lton was just outside in the hallway. I walked smack into him. He blinked as I stumbled back and then stared into a small plastic bag of candy he was holding. He didn't bolt. He didn't even look the slightest bit startled. If anything, he seemed exhausted, as if he wanted to slide right down the wall and go to sleep. I reached my hand up to my throat and gave it a gentle squeeze, reminding myself to speak.

'Is that good stuff?' I asked, nodding at the bag. 'Or is it hard candies and crap?'

'Good stuff,' he said. 'All chocolate. Is something wrong with your throat?'

I released myself from the choke hold, which had gotten tighter than I realized. Only I would strangle myself to death by accident.

'Some interesting people in there,' I said.

'Very.'

'Having fun?'

'No,' he said plainly. 'I kind of hate it. I have no idea

why. It's exotic. There's exciting people in there. Food's amazing. But it just feels like the worst night of my life. I want to get out of here, but I can't just leave.'

That was my Elton. He was demon proof.

'I guess you're pretty surprised that I'm working here, huh?'

'Not really,' he said. 'You don't exactly leave things alone. So, no. I'm not surprised you found a way in. Guess you had to see what it was all about?'

'You know me,' I said.

'Yeah.' He nodded. 'I do.'

He adjusted his shirt for a moment, and I tried not to stare at the waistband of his boxers.

'Ally really did threaten to kill herself, didn't she?' he asked.

Yes, yes, *yes*. This was the Elton I remembered. Perceptive. Relaxed. Hair half flopping, half spiking, peering over the top of his round glasses with that look he always used to give me before...

I refocused myself.

'Yes,' I said. 'She did.'

He exhaled deeply and drove his hands into his pockets.

'I'm sorry. I really am. I sort of knew it all along.'

'It must have sounded insane,' I said quietly.

'I should have believed you. I should have known you wouldn't lie about something like that. It was too much to believe. But this... this is strange.'

A door was opening. Not a literal door. The door to the ballroom remained solidly closed. I mean a door into a conversation with Elton. He may not have understood what was happening around us — no one would — but he understood that something was radically, totally wrong.

'Well, I can kind of understand,' I said slowly. 'I mean, you haven't spoken to me in six months, and *that* was the first thing we end up talking about.'

'You stopped talking to me,' he said.

This threw me a bit.

'I don't want to argue with you about this, but—'

'I wasn't going to bother you if I thought it was too hard for you,' he cut in. 'So I figured you didn't want to talk. But I would have. I thought that you were mad and that I should leave you alone.'

'For *six months*?' I shook my head.

'I thought it would be easier,' he said tiredly.

'You thought wrong. You said you wanted to be friends.'

'We were friends,' he said. 'I guess that was the problem. That was the reason for the whole thing.'

'Being *friends* with someone is not a reason to break up with them,' I said.

'It is when you realize that's all you ever will be.'

'What does *that* mean?' I asked.

'You were already getting serious. And I was worried. If we broke up after being serious, then that would be really bad. We'd both be hurt.'

He slumped. His whole body wrinkled from the utter weakness of his reason. It was the stupidest thing I'd ever heard, but he appeared to mean it. He broke up with me *to spare my feelings.*

It all became clear: when things got hard, Elton buckled. When things got serious with Ally, he just went with the easiest solution at hand. He assumed I was lying. Elton was a nice guy, but ultimately, he wasn't there when you needed him. That was the truth. That was the reality. And this was maybe the only time, ever, that it didn't really matter to me.

In that second, I was released. I felt all that heartache, all that obsessive wondering and lust and loss leave me. My mind was clear. His entire explanation was just a detail at this point, and details were irrelevant. I had a job to do, and the clock was ticking.

'Tell you what,' I said. 'You can make it up to me.'

'How?'

'Kiss me once. Now. And we'll call it even. Friends again.'

He pulled himself from the wall and looked out at the sky. The full moon was glaring at us like a big, unblinking eye.

He stepped closer. Right up to me.

'Jane...' he said.

I could feel the heat from his body. (The suit and the dancing had obviously made him warm. Really warm. Obviously sweaty warm. Had he always been this sweaty?) He didn't bend down and gently put his lips to mine. Instead, he pushed the small plastic bag into my hands.

'Here,' he said. 'Allison asked me to give this to you. She didn't think you'd get any candy because you were working. I'm here with Ally, and I... I don't do that. I don't want to do that. Okay?'

'Yeah,' I said sadly. 'I know you.'

I was going to hell because my ex-boyfriend was a decent, kind of lame guy. It was almost funny. Almost.

'I'm glad we talked,' he said.

'Yeah. Me too.'

'I'll see you around, okay?' he said. 'Really. But now, I think I have to go and get some air. I can't handle any more of those dances for a few minutes.'

He headed for the elevator, which opened for him graciously the moment he pushed the button. He leaned against the brass plates on the back wall and looked at me as the door closed, smiling lightly. There was a soft *bong*, the doors closed, and that was that.

I opened the bag and looked at my candy.

'Thanks,' I said, to no one.

That's when the owl smashed in through the window.

Chapter 37

The owl perched on a coat rack and had a look around, turning its little owl head from side to side curiously. It didn't look even mildly disturbed by the fact that it had just shattered a huge pane of glass. Not a feather was out of place. It looked at me purposefully.

'They really use owls?' I asked. 'God, she's so *bad* at this. No imagination.

It was strange, but I was suddenly feeling a little loose, kind of happy. When you pass the point of trying and enter the zone of not a chance, the pressure eases. I was going to hell in fifteen minutes. But these fifteen minutes were mine.

Lanalee emerged from the ballroom with Allison in tow. She had recovered from my attack, though her eye makeup was a bit smudged. She walked right past me with a stiff, deliberate stride and over to the bird. She extended her arm, and the bird waddled down to the end of the rack, then hopped down to her.

'We can't rely on clocks,' she said. 'When the time

comes, there's always a messenger. This is Pazuzu. Say hi.'

'Hi,' I said dully. 'How's it going?'

The owl winked hard, then fixed his eyes on me.

'Owls are great,' she said, stroking the bird's head. 'Some of them are big enough to eat house cats. Did you know that?'

Allison appeared behind her.

'You too,' Lanalee said. 'Come on.'

I guess I could have run, but I knew that would have made no difference at all. I could feel this knowledge deep down, running through my veins. All my extremities, in fact, were starting to burn and ache.

We followed her into a dank industrial stairwell that led to a heavy fire door. Then we were on the roof, right by the big neon letters that spelled out the name of the Biltmore.

'Well,' Lanalee said. 'I guess it's time to get things started!'

There was a strange brightness in the sky. The moon was heavy and orange, looking like a ripe fruit that was about to fall and splatter everywhere. Pazuzu flew over and settled himself on a pipe, ready for the show.

'You should finish your candy, Jane,' she said sympathetically. 'Never let it be said that I don't let people have their candy before I suck them dry of every shred of life and energy.'

She sat down on a vent, opened her purse, removed a lipstick, and methodically applied it without a mirror, gazing at me the whole time with her lips wide in that strange lipstick-application O shape. Allison stood in the doorway, arms folded, shivering in the cold. It was impossible to read her expression. It was a mix of her creeping blue-gray nausea face and a blank, empty stare.

I took another look at my candy. It was actually a pretty good selection of mini-candy bars — the most valuable kind of Halloween candy. It was nice of Allison to think of me, but it didn't really make up for the eternal damnation I was about to face.

But then there was an echo in my head.

I looked inside again. Candy. Candy in shiny, happy wrappers. I shook the bag a little.

'This is a very simple procedure,' Lanalee said. 'But why be simple? We need to dress this up a little. Good lighting is crucial.'

She dropped her lipstick back into her bag, then reached up and pulled out a silver slip that suspended her rust-colored hair. It dropped down her back, almost a yard of it, in one solid hair tsunami. Then she raised her hands high above her head, in the direction of the giant neon Biltmore sign.

'Lights!' she screamed.

The *B* and the *T* on the Biltmore sign buzzed and lost their power. Right above the sign, a thin rail of white lightning appeared. It squiggled a bit, as if the energy was surprised by its own freedom and excited not to be bending in the shape of a *B* and a *T*. Then it looped around, buzzed Pazuzu, and headed right for Lanalee. Despite this show, I still had one eye on the candy — my last possession, my last joy. Last, last, last. This was the end. And then I noticed something.

At the bottom, under a pile of Mr. Goodbars, was a single silver drop. It was a kiss. Hershey's Kiss. This was a kiss, given to me, by Elton.

This could not be possible. This would not work. But it was no time to comment on the *quality* of the idea. I had no other options.

'Hey,' I said. 'Um, Lanalee?'

Lanalee turned just as a pencil-thin crack of lightning landed in her upturned palm. She brushed it off her hand and blew on the spot.

'Ow! What?'

I held up the Kiss.

'Go on,' she said, looking annoyed. 'Eat it. But could you not interrupt? This is actually kind of hard.'

'It's a kiss, Lanalee. Elton gave it to me.'

The white line of light retracted like a measuring tape and the *B* and *T* were once again illuminated. Lanalee stomped over and pinched the candy from my hand. She held it right in front of her eyes and squinted at the silver wrapper as closely as a jeweller examines a diamond.

Then she looked at a spot just over my shoulder.

'What is this?' she said. 'You broke the rules. You interfered. I know you did. And this is *not* amusing.'

I turned to see Owen in the doorway, just behind Allison. He held up his hands in denial.

'No, he didn't,' Allison said, stepping forward. 'I did.'

For the first time, Lanalee was truly speechless. Silence. The *B* and *T*, overloaded and confused by the power loss and surge, made a sizzling sound and went dark with a pop, taking the *M* and the *O* with them. This left us in

236

near darkness. The moon seemed to grow larger. Allison stepped in from the doorway and stood between Lanalee and me.

'This was my fault,' she said to me. 'You were in trouble because of me. So I fixed it.'

'Fixed it?' Lanalee said, wheeling around on her. 'What do you mean, *fixed* it?'

'I played you,' Ally said, raising her head high. '*I* gave Elton the kiss and *I* told him to give it to Jane.'

'Ally…' I said.

But Ally wasn't done. She was digging her grave, but she was doing it proudly. She was taking a final stand.

'I knew you were using me to get to Jane,' she said. 'So I came back and asked you for another deal. I convinced you that I'd turn on Jane for you, make sure she went down. I set the whole thing up to make sure I lost. And now, you lose.'

The *E* crackled threateningly. It sounded like it was preparing to join its fellow defecting letters.

'See?' Ally said to me. 'I'm not so dumb.'

'I never thought you were dumb,' I said quietly.

'I did, for a long time. I thought I was weak and pathetic. But I can stand up to her.'

She indicated Lanalee with a quick jerk of her shiny red head.

'And I would never do that to you,' she added, her voice breaking. I felt my eyes fill with tears. We started toward each other, but Lanalee inserted herself between us.

'Well, well,' she said grimly. 'This is a bit of a surprise.

But I don't lose, sweetheart. I just get a second-rate prize. I'll take it anyway. And I don't feel like entertaining anyone anymore. Time to go.'

'Go where?' I asked.

'Go. Out of here.' She waved her hand around, indicating all of the city and anything beyond.

'Go?' I repeated dumbly.

Owen was grimly watching this scene unfold, his arms crossed over his chest.

'Do something,' I said weakly. 'Come on. Do something.'

'Sorry,' he said. And he really did seem sorry. 'It's just the way it is. I don't have any say. The contract is valid.'

Allison looked at him fearfully. He put his arm around her and gently led her to Lanalee, then came and stood by me.

'I have to do something,' I said.

'You tried.'

'And I failed.'

'Look,' he said. 'The rules are the rules. It's too late.'

'Sister Charles said it's never too late.'

Owen repositioned himself so that his back was to Lanalee and leaned down so that he was level with my eyes. His, I noticed, were a brilliant dollar-bill green.

'Listen to me,' he said. 'It's important that you make your own choices. There are *rules*. Remember, she has to follow the *rules* too.'

He hammered that word each time.

'Rules?' I repeated.

'It's time,' Lanalee interrupted, taking Allison by the hand. Owen and I split apart a bit, but I kept hold of one of his hands. I looked in horror at the bottle, which Lanalee was holding. She noticed this and laughed.

'I'm not really going to put her in there,' she said. 'That was a joke. I just collect bottles. Here. You can have this one.'

She tossed me the bottle.

'You might as well come with us,' Lanalee said to Owen. 'We can share a cab.'

'I guess,' he said reluctantly.

Allison slumped at the knees, so he hooked his arm through Allison's free arm to help support her.

'Where are you going?' I asked, my voice weak.

'Jane,' he said, 'remember what I just said, okay?'

Together, they went to the roof's edge. Allison made no sound. She could just about walk.

I knew in that second what they were going to do, and I almost wanted to reach out for them — grab them — but I didn't.

The two of them jumped off the roof of the hotel, taking Allison with them.

Chapter 38

The triple suicide of Owen Penderman, Allison Concord and Lanalee Tremone was the kind of thing that would rock the city of Providence, Rhode Island. Schools would close. Busloads of counselors would be carted in. Prozac would be covered in chocolate and handed out at street corners. The Biltmore would be wrapped in black cloth.

Provided it had ever happened.

After I wiped my eyes and got over the shock of seeing them all go over the edge, I walked over and peered down. There was no screaming crowd. No splotch on the sidewalk. No sound of sirens in the distance. Nothing. Nothing but a few stragglers coming and going from Halloween parties. Somewhere between the roof and the sky and the sidewalk, Lanalee, Owen, and Allison checked out.

I sat down on the edge of the building with my purple bottle, and I began to laugh. Pazuzu landed next to me and picked at the shiny candy wrappers for a moment.

When he found nothing of interest, he turned and gave me a final look, then he too departed from the roof, taking a solid plunge downward before turning sharply and disappearing around the edge of the building.

I picked at the candy. In the next five minutes, I ate every single remaining piece of chocolate. Then I went back down the grimy service steps and back to the ballroom floor. The great white doors were closed, and the whole floor was silent. I had left this room not a half hour before in the middle of a massive party. But the strangers had all vacated, taking the dogs. The lights had been brought up, and the floor was littered with balloons. Maybe half the other people were still there. The A3 were all together, lying in the center of the ballroom floor, looking at the ceiling. Cassie was twitching and laughing to herself in the corner with tears running down her face.

Donna Skal was sitting at one of the tables, staring vacantly at a balloon. She looked up at me as I entered and smiled — a large, sunny Donna smile. But nothing seemed to be behind it. I sat down next to her. It wasn't clear what was wrong with her or any of them. They may have been stunned, intoxicated, gassed… or they were just experiencing what I had already felt, the shock of knowing that a bunch of nightmarish fairy tales were real. Maybe riches or power had been dangled in front of them or visions of hell. But the bottom line was, they were checked out, all of them.

'Donna?' I said, poking at her arm.

She turned slowly and tried to focus on me.

'Jane?'

'What happened?'

'Party,' she said. 'Dance. Lots of people were talking to me.'

'What did they say?'

'They were so nice…'

'Did they try to get you to sign anything?' I asked.

'They talked about signing something…' She sighed deeply, as though all her cares in the world had settled on her like a swarm of butterflies. 'I'm going to put my head down now.'

She face-planted onto the table.

I picked up a steak knife from the table and stabbed a red balloon that had landed there. Donna didn't twitch. I sat down next to her and stroked her hair. The steak knife had gone right into the surface of the table. I had to wiggle it and pry it loose.

The door swung open, and there, heaving but otherwise intact, was Allison.

'Jane!' she said, running toward me.

'Ally? How…'

I burst into tears as she embraced me. We were both crying.

'It's a shame, isn't it?' she said.

'What?'

There was something wrong. It was Allison. It looked like Allison, sounded like Allison — but it wasn't her. I backed away.

'Surprise,' she said, giving me a slow smile. 'How do I look?'

Chapter 39

Allison-Lanalee examined the body, looking down her arms, feeling her face, checking down the front of her dress.

'It needs some work,' she said. 'But I think I can make something of it. I'll go see Paul in Boston. He's a genius with the fruit peels. Maybe a little surgery. A little TLC. It's a fixer-upper.'

'Where is she?' I growled.

'Who? Allison? She's at home, getting settled in. This is mine now. Someone will take the other body down to the river and toss it in. That girl was a swimmer. She would have wanted it that way.'

This Allison sat down, crossed her legs, and examined me in a businesslike fashion.

'So,' she said. 'That was a shocker. I feel like I've been ripped off, which I hate. I didn't think she was that smart, though I *definitely* thought she was that pathetic.'

'What are you going to do with all these people?' I

asked, ignoring this and looking over the dance floor. 'What's wrong with them?'

'Oh, they'll come around in a few. Like I said, we never use force. We do, however, know how to persuade.'

She got up and went over to the A3 and prodded them with her foot. When they didn't respond, she put her foot on Tracey's face.

'See, Jane, it's like you've always known. These are the easily led, the overly ambitious, the selfish. And while I admire that last quality... I like giving things to my friends even more. Those other people here tonight were new demons who've never harvested a soul before. I basically held this party for them. It was a banquet! We'll have all of these people under contract in no time.'

In the corner, Cassie shook until she fell to the ground. To be fair, this wasn't so far off from her normal behavior.

'Besides,' she added, 'it always annoyed me that my house, my lovely house that Fields built for me, was taken over. *I want my house back*.'

She removed her foot from Tracey and stretched.

'I have to go,' she said. 'I have people coming over to talk business. You enjoy yourself, Jane. And if you ever change your mind, just give a shout. I'll be listening.'

She vamped her way across the room and was gone.

All of these people would be taken. This was just the beginning. And Allison was gone.

I sat there for some time, hugging my knees to my chest, until the door creaked open once more and my sister's head of long, glossy hair peered around it.

'Jane!' She ran over and embraced me. This time, I

244

knew it was real. This was Joan, smelling overpoweringly of hair-care products and raspberry gum. I hugged her back, tight.

'You are so hard-core!' she said. 'I called Carbo and he told me that the whole staff had been kicked out. I can't believe it! Mom and Dad are so worried, though. You have to come home. I can't handle it anymore.'

She looked around at the carnage.

'These people are so drunk! Why didn't you tell me you were going to a party?'

'It kind of sucked,' I said. 'You wouldn't have liked it.'

'Is this why you wouldn't go to that school in Boston today?'

'Kind of.'

'That,' she said solemnly, 'is the best thing I have ever heard.'

She hugged me again, and I held on for dear life.

'Joan,' I said, not letting go, 'what do you do when demons come?'

'What?'

'Say you were in a TV show and demons attacked your school. What would you do?'

Joan leaned back and gave this all of her thought.

'Well, that depends,' she said. 'What am I? Do I have powers? Am I a witch?'

'Nope.'

'Well,' she said. 'Aren't you just supposed to kill them?'

'What if you couldn't kill them?'

'Why can't you kill them?'

'Because they'll...' I wasn't sure, actually. Probably

something bad. No matter what, killing this demon meant killing Allison, even if it was just her body. And then what? Kill all those people?

'Just killing them isn't an option. They're hard to kill. And there are too many of them.'

'Well, then, you vanquish them!'

TV had really improved my sister's vocabulary.

'How?' I asked.

'With a spell. You trick them.'

'What if you don't have a spell?'

'Well, what do you have?' she asked.

I looked around. I had nothing. I had me. I had the steak knife. I held it up.'

'You have this,' I said.

Joan looked at it critically.

'That's not going to kill a demon,' she said. 'This isn't a very good show.'

'No,' I said, carefully holding the knife out at arm's length, 'it's not.'

'But it would be a good show if you were the one fighting them,' Joan said, fluffing my spikes gently. 'Are you the one fighting them?'

'Yeah,' I said into her leg. 'I fight the demons.'

Actually, I realized, I was doing no such thing. I *had* tried to figure my way through this, and I had failed — or I had succeeded to the point where I was alive and safe, but my best friend was not. My best friend had gone down trying to keep me from saving her.

I could have walked away then. I could take my chips and go home. But a very loose idea began to form in my mind. Well, sort of an outline of a possible idea. It was in what Owen had told me — *Lanalee had to follow the rules too.*

And suddenly, I understood what I had to do. The outline became a rising impulse that pulled me up.

I looked over at my sister, who was fiddling with the ends of her hair, still thinking on the problem.

'Joan,' I said, 'I want you to know two things. You're the best sister in the world, and they don't really have flying cars in Japan.'

'I never believed that,' Joan said, undisturbed. 'I stopped believing all that stuff when you told me that India used to be a part of England.'

'That one is true,' I said. 'It was an empire.'

'Yeah, right. And did it strike back?'

'Joan,' I said. 'I have to go. And I could be home really, really late. But just remember that, okay? The thing about being the best sister.'

'Where are you going?' she asked. 'Can I come?'

I reached out and hugged her hard again.

'No,' I said. 'I have to go alone. Go home, Joan. Get out of here.'

'But you'll come back home, right?' she said.

I hesitated.

'As soon as I can,' I said, trying to keep my voice firm.

When she was gone, I took a deep breath and scrawled a message on a piece of napkin. This was my last chance to walk away.

I went back to the roof.

Chapter 40

The first part was calling the hell back down on myself, and that meant I needed the bird.

'Pazuzu!' I screamed into the night sky. 'Get back here!'

I retrieved the purple bottle and carefully rolled up the napkin scrap and threaded it into the small hole. By the time I had done this, I saw that the owl had rejoined me. He was sitting quietly on a bent antenna.

'Listen up, bird,' I said.

Pazuzu cocked his head.

'I have a message for your owner,' I said. 'You're going to take it to her.'

Pazuzu looked a little put out by my demand; he pulled his head back a bit. Still, he dutifully sideways waddled down the antenna to me, reached out with one taloned foot, and deftly took the bottle from my grasp.

'Thanks,' I added.

He shot into the air, the bottle dangling freely beneath him. He dove over the edge of the building.

About a minute passed during which I did nothing but dumbly stare at the *B* on the Biltmore sign. It hummed.

Suddenly, there was an incredible snap of cold — like that feeling in the dead of summer when you walk past a store and get that blast of air-conditioning — that, but about a hundred times more intense. It burned my skin. Suddenly a split appeared in the sky, a painful red cut. Pazuzu flew out of this, and the cold seemed to be sucked back into this wound as it closed itself. Pazuzu flew overhead, dropped the bottle back into my outstretched hands, then sat back on the antenna and preened himself.

I pulled the stopper from the bottle and removed the scrap. Right under my message, I saw the following words, scrawled in the familiar ornate, looping hand:

My house in five minutes. Don't be late.

'Five minutes?' I said out loud. 'How am I supposed to get there in five minutes?'

Pazuzu pulled his face out of his own feathers and cocked his head at me, as if puzzling this over himself. Then he blinked his yellow eyes and fixed them on a point just behind me.

I turned to see Mr. Fields standing on the very edge of the rooftop, his back facing the open sky and the moon.

'Nice to see you again, Jane!' he said, bowing low. 'Come alone. My car is waiting.'

He didn't move from the roof edge. Instead, he slipped off his glasses and replaced them with a pair of old-fashioned goggles — massive ones, like the kind people used to wear to go 'motoring.'

'The stairs are this way,' I said, pointing to the door.

'No time.' He fussed with the goggles with one hand and waved me toward him with the other. 'No need. Come along.'

'Come along where?'

'To Mistress!' he said brightly. 'Come along now.'

He reached out to me. This could mean only one thing.

'No,' I said. 'I'll take the stairs.'

'If you want to talk to Mistress, this is the only way,' he said primly, as if he was admonishing a small child. 'Come now.'

There was no going back. Only forward. I joined him on the edge.

'Now,' he said, 'I should warn you that sometimes this hurts a bit.'

With the slightest of tugs, I felt my heels liberated from the surface.

Maybe you've wondered what it's like to fall off a tall building. Well, let me fill you in.

The first second is really, really good. It's surprisingly like the cartoons, where the fateful character hovers for a moment after running off the cliff. Everything is still. There's no cold or restriction…You're just free. For just a second, you really feel like you're standing on air.

And then you realize that you are not. This is not as fun.

The falling is pretty much what you might imagine. You fall. It happens very quickly and you have no real time to be scared because you are simply flattened by the force of falling until your face feels like a pancake.

What I didn't expect was the fact that you flip over and go headfirst. Then you get this feeling like every single internal organ and bone in your body just slips out of place and lodges somewhere in your neck. The blood really does rush to your head, causing a sensation a little bit like drinking fifty cups of coffee in one second might feel if that was possible. My arms were flapping uselessly at my sides, rubbery as fish fins. I knew I had to be nauseous — it would come when my body understood gravity again. Next to me, Mr. Fields was in pretty much the same position, but he was holding his arms back gracefully and putting his smiling face against the wind. He was shouting something, but I couldn't hear him.

There was ground coming up fast now. I was ten feet, five feet, four, knee-high distance. I could see the pattern of the concrete clearly. Then my legs bent around hard, arching my body completely. I tumbled in the air, turning the right way around. I landed heels first. The sidewalk was solid — it made my teeth chatter — but it didn't kill me.

Mr. Fields was standing next to me. His little silver sports car was waiting, engine running, right next to where we had landed. I looked around, expecting to see crowds of terrified Halloween revelers or at least a startled doorman. But there was no one. It was just an empty stretch of sidewalk. Not abandoned. There was just no one there at that second. I got the feeling this was not a coincidence.

Mr. Fields ushered me to the car and settled me into the front seat. My entire body, I noticed, was now shuddering with the most painful cold. Anticipating this need, he tucked a purple cashmere lap blanket over me.

'That happens,' he said. 'That feeling of cold. It's because you have a soul and a life force. When you do something like jump off a building, it starts to slip away. It'll snap back into place in a moment.'

He hurried around and got in on the driver's side. He fumbled with the stereo for a moment, then he was blasting Beethoven and the whole car was groaning with the heavy-belly sound of cellos. Then we were speeding off down the empty streets, with the other cars always just a block or two in the distance but never in our way.

The sports car loved the challenge of the Providence ski slope hills, and the engine purred happily as it pulled us up the streets. Maybe two minutes later, we were coming to a checkered-flag stop in front of Lanalee's, right behind a line of silver cars.

'Houseful tonight,' Mr. Fields said pleasantly. 'Well, here you are. Good luck, my dear. We're all very happy to have you with us.'

It was cold now. For reasons I have never quite understood, cold always makes things louder. My shoe made a definite crunch as it made contact with the pavement. Pazuzu was there already, sitting placidly on a yellow porch light, occasionally pecking at the bulb. I could hear a lot of noise coming from inside. It sounded like the party had simply moved here.

In case you're thinking that I'm exceptionally

brave — don't be fooled. I wasn't happy about any of this. I definitely wasn't looking forward to going smack into a house full of demons. But there are times in life when only one path is presented to you. The path may be rocky, on fire, populated by poisonous cottonmouth snakes... but it's your path.

Chapter 41

The door wasn't locked, so I just went in. The foyer was empty, but the Tremone living room was packed. The air was smoky, with a light touch of cloves. I recognized most of the people from the prom. David was stretched out on a sofa, looking elegant in a consumptive, low-red-blood-cell-count kind of way.

Allison stepped through the crowd, which parted graciously to make way for her. Some people reached out to stroke her red hair, to touch her dress.

'Hi, shortie,' she said. 'Snack?'

'We need to talk,' I said.

'Food first,' she said. 'I have things here tonight you wouldn't believe. Sushi that Tokyo would die for. And these smoked almonds from Seville that would make any self-respecting Spaniard eat his own arm off in envy. Try.'

She popped a smoked almond in my mouth. I almost choked on it and started coughing. She slapped my back.

'Careful, Jane. Death by tapas sounds like a good way to go, but not on my carpet. Now, what brings you here? Did my very generous offer tempt you?'

'No,' I said. 'I've just come to tell you that you were wrong.'

A snicker spread across the room.

'Oh, Jane,' she said. 'Please don't. Don't try to wheedle your way through by saying I didn't give her what she really wanted or something lame like that. My contract is airtight. You won. She lost. End of Allison. Buh-bye and thanks for playing.'

'She came back to you to save me. She made sure you lost.'

'That,' Lanalee said, 'is because she's a *loser*. Seriously, Jane, you're bringing the room down. Have something to eat. Have you ever had baby octopus? Looks scary, but you've never had anything like it. Or maybe...'

She reached her arm back. Through the crowd, a cupcake was passed, hand over hand, to her. She held it in front of me. It was red velvet, with deep red icing to boot. I turned away from it.

'Your favorite. Go on.'

'All of you,' I said, turning to the crowd. 'You all came here for something, right? You were all promised things. You're all going to follow someone who can't give you what you want?'

Lanalee smiled slowly, but there was no contentment in it.

'They know better,' she said.

'Do they? What did you give them? Poodle Prom?

Free run of Rhode Island? What, was *Lichtenstein* already taken?'

This quieted the room.

'Are you expecting all of these people to follow you from now on?' I asked. 'Because you gave them some Catholic school girls from Providence? Is that the best you can do, Miss I'm a Big Scary Demon?'

'Sorry,' she said, turning her attention to some cupcakes on the table. 'Kind of bored now, Jane. You can go.'

There was some mumbling now, and some in the crowd were looking at Lanalee with some uncertainty. Lanalee herself seemed quite sure of what she had just said.

'Not just yet,' I said, 'there's one more thing.'

'Oh?' she said, licking all the frosting from a cupcake and setting it back on the tray. 'What's that?'

'I…' I pulled the knife from my pocket. 'Have the steak knife of righteousness.'

'The wha…'

It was the open-toed shoes that made it so easy — that and the knife itself — and maybe the fact that in the end it's true… the stressed person can lift a car off a child or slice through human bone. The toes came right off. I dropped to my knees and took them all, all ten, as easy as slicing a pat of butter. I was trying for the big ones, but I ended up getting them all in one solid chop.

'How are you going to lead them now?' I said.

Lanalee looked down at it in shock… and then, she began to topple. She went backward onto one of the sofas and looked down at her mangled feet. There was a lot of blood — it ran out of her feet and right into the red carpet, where it left a darkened pool.

There was a lot of screaming and profanity from Lanalee for the next few minutes. I've heard some good profanity in my time, but you just can't compare to a pissed-off demon for that.

I stood in the center of the room, surrounded by demons, holding a bloody knife — and I had just cut off all of Satan's assistant's toes, my best friend's toes...I had cut off ten toes, and no matter how you broke that down, it meant that I was *in it* now.

Lanalee managed to find the will to speak. She was out of breath, almost hissing.

'You think that's going to do it?' she asked. 'You think I'll give her back just because you mangled her?'

Well, actually, I had wondered if that would work. A tiny part of me had hoped that Lanalee would lose her balance and say, 'Now it's useless! You broke it!' and fly out of Allison's body in a puff of smoke. But no. I was going to have to go through with the whole plan.

'So, Jarvis the Genius,' she said, her voice wobbling, 'what's your next move?'

Lanalee was running pale right up through Allison's forehead — I could see that through the red bangs. Poor Allison. What had I done to her? Why had she ended up like this?

The other guests moved quietly to the side of the room to watch this play out. They made no move toward me, toward Lanalee or Allison. They just watched as their hostess writhed in pain and then fell heaving against the back of the sofa.

'I'm going to let her die,' she said.

'She won't die…' I said, looking at the still-bleeding wounds. 'It's just toes.'

'Oh, she will, though. She'll bleed to death if I don't do anything. And I'm not going to do anything. I'm going to sit here.'

She folded her arms over her chest and set her expression, like she was *concentrating* on bleeding.

'The human body goes into shock when it loses too much blood,' she went on. 'The circulatory system collapses. It doesn't take that much to kill a human. She'll die. I'm going to make you a murderer — unless you want to save me? Want to save me, Jane? Want to keep me alive?'

She was getting pale now, her skin turning the familiar blue-bready color.

'So what's it going to be?' she said. 'You going to call an ambulance? Let me go on? Or are you going to let Allison bleed to death?'

'You're not Allison,' I said in a low voice.

'But this is her body. And that's her blood ruining my gorgeous carpet. They don't make carpets like this anymore. What a shame.'

She managed to pull her lips into a grin. David came a little closer and peered down over my shoulder.

'I kind of want to follow you,' he said. 'What do you do?'

'Get something to wrap her feet in,' I said. 'We need to stop the bleeding.'

'You stabbed her, Mistress.'

'Yes, I *know* I stabbed her. Now get towels or something! And don't call me Mistress.'

David seemed to be the type who liked commands, and he ran off eagerly and returned a moment later with a pile of luxurious amber-colored towels — heavy Egyptian cotton things, big as blankets.

'Oh,' Lanalee said, her strength wavering, 'what a hero. Jane to the rescue... Jane the pure.'

'Grab her foot hard,' I said, ignoring her and grabbing a towel and hugging one of Al's poor mangled feet. 'Put pressure on the wound.'

The blood came fast, filling the towel. I pressed harder.

'What are you going to do?' David asked.

'I'm thinking,' I said.

Lanalee gave me one last look of total disdain, and then her head fell back against the sofa and her eyes shut.

The group around us had watched this with curiosity up to this point. But when Lanalee passed out, they must have gotten the idea that nothing would be forthcoming to them, and they began to drift off. There was a herd mentality — when one left, another would notice and decide to leave too. In only a few minutes, Lanalee's friends had left her, toeless and unconscious. Only David remained.

Allison's toes were on the carpet. They were so small now that they were detached. They reminded me of mushrooms — little gray mushrooms. With red stuff on them. I reeled and grabbed the other foot from David.

'Plastic bag,' I said, turning away. 'Ice. Pick those up. Put them in the bag. Put them in the refrigerator.'

'Are you going to eat them?' he said eagerly.

Now I could see why Lanalee stored this guy in the tub. I shot him a look, and he got moving.

'Okay, Lanalee,' I said, holding fast to her feet. 'No more deals. No more souls on the line. All your friends have left you. But I'm going to help you. I'm going to save you. I'm even going to save your stupid toes.'

I grabbed both feet in one hand. The phone was on the side table, next to the sofa, so I had to stand up carefully. As I leaned over Lanalee to get the phone and was talking to the operator, she opened her eyes, looked directly at me. I felt her hand on mine.

I think I laughed when the knife went in. At least, I made the motion, but blood came out of my mouth instead. I remember seeing the perfume bottles on the mantelpiece as I fell back and, aside from the faint, somewhat implausible realization that I was dying, nothing else.

And I smiled.

'Got you,' I said.

Chapter 42

The entire horizon was white. White, and a strip of blue, and a gray cloud in the distance. A very square cloud. My mind was thick with clouds. They hung over all my thoughts like cobwebs, gumming everything up and slowing everything down, but I didn't mind.

'Jane?'

Whose voice was that?

And the air… it had the faintest smell of… green beans? Chicken? Antiseptic spray?

I made a tremendous effort and pulled my eyes open wider.

That gray thing was a television. A wall-mounted television. The white-and-blue landscape was a pillow in my face. I was sleeping with my mouth open, and I had a little plug stuck in my nose that was shooting cool air into it. It annoyed me, and I yanked it out. A hand reached over and put it back into place. I pulled it out again, and the hand replaced it. The hand and I battled like this for another few moments — it very much wanted that plug in my nose. And though the air that it supplied was cool and pleasant, I was determined that the plug was going to stay out.

There were footsteps. Distant voices talking about doctors. This was definitely a hospital. I remembered now — something had been in my chest. My chest was thick and fluffy. Those were bandages. I had been hurt. I had been stabbed in the chest. By a demon. At a party.

That didn't help my confusion. I started clawing through those webs in my head, trying to untangle my thoughts. Something about falling off a building and slicing off toes…None of it made sense.

Neither did the large pink thing that was standing over me, shoving the plug back into my nose. After a fuzzy moment, this resolved itself into a nurse with a long blond ponytail and the darkest tan I've ever seen in a New England autumn. She looked a little like Joan, actually.

'You're awake!' she said. 'I'm amazed.'

Was I awake? I couldn't quite figure it out.

'You're a miracle,' she said, stroking my hair, 'you know that? Everyone on the unit is calling this the miracle of the month. Full moon on Halloween. We knew we were going to see something incredible.'

I tried to move my mouth, but something was preventing me.

'Don't try to talk, honey,' she said. 'There was a tube down your throat earlier, when you were in surgery. It's probably sore.'

My throat did burn, but it didn't feel like it had had a tube down it. More like a string of fishhooks and lit matches.

'I know you don't feel good,' she said sympathetically. 'I'll go and get you something to help you get back to sleep. But first, have a look.'

The nurse pulled back the curtain that surrounded us. There, in the next bed, was Ally, sleeping soundly, her large forehead resting peacefully on a pillow. She also had a plug in her nose, a plastic mask over her mouth, and tubes coming out of her arms.

'She lost a lot of blood,' she said. 'But she'll be okay. They got the two of you here in the nick of time. They even managed to re-attach all of her toes. She'll probably limp, but it's better than the alternative.'

Now it was coming back to me.

They got the guy who did this to you two,' she said. 'Don't worry. The police found him at the scene mumbling about the devil. He even had your friend's toes in a bag. You're safe now, honey.'

Poor stupid David.

So there she was. Alive. But who was I looking at? There's no way that the nurse could have understood the true meaning of my searching gaze. There was no physical sign.

'Someone's coming by to switch on your television,' the nurse said, pulling the curtain closed. 'You won't want it now. You're still groggy. But your parents might want it. Try to rest now, okay? I'm going to get you some medicine. You'll go right back to sleep.'

After reading the monitors around me and making a few notes, she left. I was vaguely aware that a tall guy in a work uniform came in and started doing something to my television.

'I couldn't tell you directly,' he said, not turning around. 'I couldn't tell you exactly what you had to do. But I knew you would figure it out.'

My eyes shot open. From under the baseball cap he was wearing, a tiny tuft of red hair was peeking out.

I tried to speak, but the burning, blistered feeling prevented me.

'I don't have a lot of time,' he said, coming over. 'Brother Frank got your parents out of the room for a minute.'

Did it work? I tried to ask with my eyes. *Who is that?*

Owen seemed to understand.

'It's the first forfeit I've ever seen,' he said with a smile.

Allison?

'It's her,' he said. 'You did it. You got her to break the rules. You made her mad enough to attack a human being. She's *never* done that before. Not only was Allison returned, but Lanalee probably got knocked all the way down the ladder. Two hundred years of work for nothing. She's going to be *pissed.*'

Allison. That was Allison. My best friend, who had given herself up for me.

And Owen was here.

'I was scared,' he said. 'I mean, I'm dead. I've died twice. I know it's no big deal, but I didn't...'

Owen was finding it hard to contain his emotions. He

broke out into the broadest smile I'd ever seen and was gripping the bed rail so hard that it shook. He reached down and took my hand, carefully avoiding the tubes and the tape.

'I couldn't watch you go there. Put yourself in danger. I made sure Brother Frank was there watching, to call an ambulance. And they all took off, Jane. All of them ran, left town. They always come back, but that doesn't matter. We beat them this time, Jane. You guys made it.'

He was rambling now, running his fingers up and down the bed rail. It's possible that I was on serious painkillers and slightly loopy, but Owen didn't seem to be the same guy I had known all along. The height, the skinny body, the thin lips and vampire eyebrows were all still the same. Something had changed, though. I couldn't put my finger on it even as he leaned down over me.

'I'm not supposed to do this either,' he said. 'But these are different rules, and I've waited a long time for this.

Owen did not kiss like a freshman. He kissed firmly, seriously. He kissed like someone who has been around a long, long time and who has waited patiently for this very moment. I suddenly understood how some things only improve with time, how nothing is lost in the passing. Any kiss I shared with Elton paled in comparison to this. There was an entire century of experience and emotion behind this one.

This was it. The big romantic moment of my life had come, and my partner was a 116-year-old dead fourteen-year-old freshman. But hey, don't know it until you've tried it. That's my motto.

'I have to go,' he said, pulling away. 'They'll be back any second.'

Granted, he wasn't about to leap off a building again, but somehow… this made it worse. I couldn't let Owen go. But I couldn't speak. So I just grasped his hand and held on.

'Jane,' he said, 'you just beat Lanalee. Brother Frank is never going to let you get away. You're with us now.'

I clung to his fingers with all the might I could.

'Besides,' he said, carefully withdrawing them from my grip, 'I've been waiting a long time for a girlfriend. I'm not just going to give you up. You'll see me again. But right now, you have to go *to sleep*.'

As he said the words, I felt my body shudder with exhaustion. Maybe I was asleep already. I could barely keep my eyes open as I watched him straighten his cap, pick up the toolbox, and go.

I'm shocked that any story about me would end like this, but there you go. Nothing like a fight with a demon, a dead boyfriend, and a stab wound to the chest to put things into perspective.

I turned and tried to gaze through the curtain that Allison was resting behind. I could just make out her figure on the bed. There would be a lot of questions to answer. People would want to know what happened in the Tremone house tonight.

Outside, the sky was clear and flat and bright. The moon was still high. I could hear Brother Frank, my parents, and Joan as they walked back toward the room. Providence, capitol of the State of Rhode Island and Providence Plantations, had been saved from an infestation of demons.

And I was going to get a well-deserved night's sleep.

Acknowledgments

Professionally and personally, many thanks to: Ben Schrank, Josh Bank, Les Morgenstein, Siobhan Vivian, Eloise Flood, Liesa Abrams, Kate Schafer, and Hamish Young.

Jack the Ripper returns...

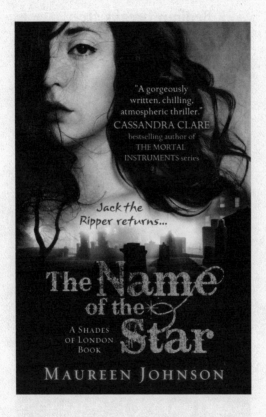

'A gorgeously written, chilling, atmospheric thriller.'
CASSANDRA CLARE

Out now

Bedlam breaks free...

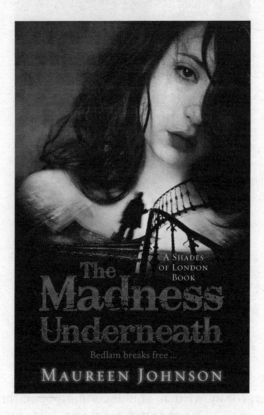

Coming soon in January 2013